MW01634081

GUARDING AMBERLEY (SPECIAL FORCES: OPERATION ALPHA)

Guardian Seals Book 8

NICOLE FLOCKTON

This book is a work of fiction. Names, characters, places, and incidents are products of the author's imagination or used fictitiously. Any resemblance to actual events or locales or persons living or dead is entirely coincidental.

Dear Readers,

Welcome to the Special Forces: Operation Alpha Fan-Fiction world!

If you are new to this amazing world, in a nutshell the author wrote a story using one or more of my characters in it. Sometimes that character has a major role in the story, and other times they are only mentioned briefly. This is perfectly legal and allowable because they are going through Aces Press to publish the story.

This book is entirely the work of the author who wrote it. While I might have assisted with brainstorming and other ideas about which of my characters to use, I didn't have any part in the process or writing or editing the story.

I'm proud and excited that so many authors loved my characters enough that they wanted to write them into their own story. Thank you for supporting them, and me!

READ ON!

Xoxo

Susan Stoker

To my bestie Abigail who's been on this crazy ride with me since 2016.

I couldn't do half of what I've done without you!

ACKNOWLEDGEMENTS

Once again a huge thank you to Susan for letting me play in her world and use her characters. This series maybe over but it's not the end of our journey together.

With each book I thank my readers and this one is no different. While the Guardian Seals stories may be over, I won't be able to keep these boys from making guest appearances. Thank you all for taking a risk on me and starting with Protecting Lily and staying with me until we reached Red's story. I appreciate each and every one of you.

Abigail, you are the best friend and writing partner a girl could have. Even recovering from surgery you were able to give me your insight and help.

Jennifer, again you created a wonderful cover for

me. We continue to travel this road in publishing together and I'm so glad we are.

Margaret, thanks for beta reading this book for me. Appreciate your insight, even though we do have such different styles LOL.

Finally, to my family, thank you always for supporting and loving me.

CHAPTER ONE

TEAM CAP ALL THE WAY.

Amberley Price bit back a smile as she typed the message under the table. Texting Thomas Grant was the only way she could get through this dinner. A few seconds later her phone vibrated and she covertly glanced at the screen under the table.

I DON'T THINK WE CAN BE FRIENDS ANYMORE. #TEAMSTARK FOR THE WIN.

Swallowing down a snort, she fired off another response.

REALLY? SHOULDN'T YOU BE ALL TEAM CAPTAIN AMERICA CONSIDERING HE'S THE DEFENDER OF ALL MEN ?

"Have you given anymore thought about that screenplay I sent you, dear," her mother's voice penetrated, bringing her back to the dinner table. "I think you'd be perfect to play the lead role. It's almost like it was written with you in mind. Rob, here, is already slated to play the lead male role."

Amberley head jolted up, laid her phone on her lap, and shoved another forkful of Beef Wellington into her mouth so she didn't have to answer. The second she'd walked into her parents' Beverly Hills mansion she'd suspected her mom and dad were up to their match-making scheme again. Once a week she had dinner with them and over the last two months there had been an extra guest. Always a single guy. Always in the industry. Always eager to please Amberley.

God, how many times did she have to tell her parents, she wasn't looking for a long term relationship. Her main focus was on her career as a screenwriter, which gave her mother, big screen icon Bettina Price, heart palpitations.

Prices belong on the big screen. We always have. We don't belong behind the scenes where the limelight doesn't shine.

As if it wasn't hard enough growing up in Beverly Hills, it was ten times harder when you came from Hollywood royalty. Her mom and dad had fallen in love on a movie set, just like her maternal grandparents.

It's in the blood, her mom kept prattling on. Well, it wasn't in her blood. Amberley preferred to be out of the limelight and work her magic with her laptop. Create beautiful stories so actors, who weren't her, could bring them to life.

"Did you hear your mother, Amberley?" Her father's stern tone suggested only one thing—answer or be banished to her room without dessert, like she was fifteen again. The threat didn't work then and it wasn't going to work now.

"I heard, Dad, but as I've told you and Mom on numerous occasions, I don't want to take any acting roles. Not anymore. My acting career is over." She looked up in time to see Rob's eyebrows rise in surprise at her declaration.

Of course, it didn't help that for a few years as a pre-teen, she'd succumbed to family history and had a role in a very successful TV sitcom. A show that still netted her the occasional residual check, thanks to streaming services having picked it up. Not enough income to live off, but always a lovely bonus when it came in.

It had been fun at the time, and for a short while she'd enjoyed being famous. Like the saying, *all that glitters is not gold,* being famous became a chore. Finding friends who liked her for who she was and not her name was even more difficult. Now that her life was not in front of the camera anymore she couldn't be happier.

Her mother sighed. "Oh Amberley, that's such a huge mistake. You could be making so much more money if you'd just let go of this silly little dream of yours to write."

This script she was writing had to be a success, if not her parents would up the ante in their *Amberley Must Act* program. There was one thing her parents hadn't learned about her, or refused to acknowledge, was that no matter how much they pushed, she wasn't going to fall in line with their wishes.

Her phone vibrated and she forced herself not to pick it up. Although it was tempting, her mom certainly wouldn't be happy if she did.

"I think it's important to follow your dreams. I know I wouldn't be where I am if I'd listened to my parents. They wanted me to join the family construction business." Rob piped up beside her.

Even though there was no chance in hell she'd hook up with the guy, she was grateful he was trying to show her support. She smiled at him in thanks and he returned it with one of his own.

There was no zing of attraction between them. No spark of need to jump across the table and rip his clothes off. The way Rob was looking at her, it was clear he felt the same way. Most of the other guys her parents had tried to set her up with attempted to make love to her feet with their own. Rob kept his firmly on his side of the table.

How many numbers had she had to block after these dinners? Too many to count. Two of the *dates* her parents had invited weren't even big named stars, they were wannabes playing at the big time. Amberley still couldn't understand why her mom presented those guys to her. One guy had been so persistent she'd threatened him with a restraining order to stop calling her. It had been a couple of months since she'd last heard from him—thank goodness.

"Well I'm glad you didn't listen to your parents. The world would be a poorer place without the talented Rob Gregor gracing our screens." Her mom sent him her I'm-a-star smile.

Geez, could Mom lay it on any thicker? She looked at Rob as if he was the greatest thing since sliced bread. Luckily Rob was taking it all in his stride.

"That's very kind of you, Mrs. Price, but the words are what make my job easy. If it wasn't for the skill of the screenwriters, then I wouldn't have the material to work with."

Rob was definitely ticking all the boxes when it came to dealing with her mom. Not to mention supporting her. In a couple of sentences, he'd managed to validate her career. A career that was beginning to take off. Pity she just didn't find him attractive. Now if it was Thomas Grant, well then that would be different.

Placing her knife and fork on her plate she rested her hands in her lap, on her phone. Pulling it to the side she unlocked it and read Thomas's message.

Clearly you don't understand the sacrifices Stark makes over all the movies. Our friendship was beautiful while it lasted.

She snorted, holding it back was impossible. She fired off a quick response.

Shame, lately I've been finding military guys ... fun ;)

"Amberley, are you texting at the table?"

Busted.

"Sorry, Mom, I was just, um, talking to someone about the script I'm writing. It's an action adventure move involving—"

"I've taught you better. Don't text at the table."

Well if Rob was any type of interested in her before, he wasn't now. Not with her being reprimanded like a child. If he hadn't been sitting right there she'd strongly remind her mother that she was a grown woman.

Geez, she couldn't wait to leave and get back to her words.

"Well, Mr. and Mrs. Price it's been wonderful but I've got an early call tomorrow, so I'm afraid I'm going to have to leave." Rob pushed his chair out and stood.

"I'll see you out, Rob." Amberley repeated the action. That's the least she could do seeing as he'd given her support when her mom got onto her career high horse.

They reached the front door and a glance down the hallway showed her mom peeking around the corner.

Oh my God, she never gives up.

Amberley waved her hand in a shooing motion, hoping her mom got the message. She really needed to put some space between her and her parents. Maybe a research trip for her new script was called for. Immediately a vision of Thomas flashed in her mind. He'd been so helpful and as she was getting deeper into the script his insight would be invaluable. Maybe he'd be open to her visiting in person instead of exchanging messages.

"I have to say this evening was rather different." Rob's words pulled her back to the present.

She smiled, glad he could find humor in a difficult dinner. "God, I'm so sorry. My mom thinks because she and dad fell in love on a movie set that I'm destined to as well. Unfortunately, you got dragged into it."

Rob chuckled. "Yeah, I kind of worked that out." He leaned closer to her. "I didn't want to break your mom's heart, but I don't think my boyfriend would appreciate me stepping out on him."

Amberley looked up at Rob in shock. "You're gay? I had no idea." Growing up in Hollywood, she had plenty of gay friends, she just hadn't had a clue with Rob.

He shrugged. "I don't talk about my sexuality. It's no one's business. When the time is right, I'll come out to the world. I'm looking at a movie now which could be the stepping stone to that announcement."

She placed her hand over her heart. "I promise your secret is safe with me. Thanks again for standing up to my mom, it doesn't happen often."

Rob bent and pressed a soft kiss against her cheek. "I believe it's important for people to follow what their heart desires. If acting isn't that for you and screenwriting is, go for it. Just let me know when you've written a script you think would work for me. I'd love to be part of it."

Amberley opened the door. "Thanks Rob. And I will definitely send something to you when I have it. How do you feel about action and adventure movies?"

"I'm always up for a challenge. I'll see you around, Amberley."

"Bye, Rob."

Amberley tracked his movements down the stairs that would rival the staircase Cinderella fled down as midnight struck. It would be doubtful that Rob would leave behind a glass slipper.

No wonder there was no spark between them, she pondered as she closed the door. No chance of him being interested in her at all. Sadly, having to convince her mom that the chances of her becoming Mrs. Rob Gregor was about as likely as her winning an Oscar for acting. Now an Oscar for best original screenplay, that was her dream. Whatever her mom said, or how much she tried to convince Amberley to pursue Rob, she would keep his secret.

When the news came out it would no doubt break a lot of female hearts. Then again there could be many young teenage boys who would be thrilled with the news.

Time to face the firing squad. She couldn't keep hanging out in the foyer. Sighing, she closed the door and walked to the living room. She had to come up with something to stop them in their matchmaking steps.

She was going to be a screenwriter, wasn't she?

Surely she could come up with a plausible and believable story that would get them off her back.

As she paused outside the room, she wished for a fairy godmother to get her out of her dilemma. And boy, she really needed to drop the Disney references. Besides she could save herself, she didn't need anyone's help.

Straightening her shoulders, she walked into the living room. "Mom, how many times do I have to tell you, please stop with the matchmaking attempts, it's getting old and I'm never going to hook up with one of your suitable suitors."

Her mother waved away her concerns. "I'm doing nothing of the kind. I'm just inviting colleagues over for dinner. Although I do think Rob is a lovely man and would be perfect for you. You would be a Hollywood power couple for sure. Did I mention he's the lead in the movie of the script I sent you?"

Now why didn't that shock her? Of course, he would be. She sat on the couch. Her mom didn't like her standing while arguing with her. "I don't care, Mom. I've told you I'm not going back into acting. I've been there, done that and don't really want to do it again. I want the freedom to be able to go shopping when and where I want. I don't want to be recognized all the time."

Acting was behind her and now she was an independent woman, who had a script to write. A research trip to see Thomas was looking like a fabulous idea.

Thomas. If only there was more between them than just texts. It definitely wouldn't be a hardship. He's filled out nicely since he became a SEAL. I bet he can squat while holding an eight foot plank of wood across his shoulders.

Hmm, maybe her inner voice was on to something. No, it was a bad idea, she shouldn't go with it. It really wasn't a sensible thing to do.

But it would get your mother off her matchmaking track if she knew you had a boyfriend.

Yeah, but her mom wanted her with an A-Class actor as a boyfriend, not a man who couldn't catapult Amberley's star higher into the stratosphere.

"Amberley, sweetheart, we've tried to support your little escapade into screenwriting, but I've seen screenwriters come and go. I think you need to reconsider what you're doing. And I strongly believe your future lies with making movies. Every movie you star in will be a box office smash. You come from Hollywood royalty, darling."

Amberley clenched her fists to stop herself from grabbing the thousand dollar decorative pillow next to her and throwing it at her mother. "Mom, stop it. I'm not fifteen anymore." She stood up, making a decision. "Honestly, your support hasn't been all that supportive.

And your lack of faith is hurtful. While you may not believe in my screenwriting abilities, Trident Movies, and Pascal Hernandez do. I'm writing the screen play for Pascal's new action adventure movie, and I'm going out of town for the next couple of weeks on a research trip."

"What? Pascal Hernandez asked you to write a movie?" Her father blurted out. It took a lot to make John Price sit up and listen, naming one of the hottest directors in Hollywood would do it every time.

"Yes, Dad he did. He personally phoned me and told me about the ideas he had and asked me to come up with a short sample for him to read. I did that and he liked where I was headed. He asked me to write the whole thing, which I've been doing over the last month. I'm very excited and I would appreciate your support."

"Why didn't you say something sooner?" Her mother asked.

"If you'd taken an interest at all in what I'm doing, you'd know that the scripts I've written for some independent movies have been praised. But you've ignored all that because all you want is for me it to do what you want and go back into acting. You need to understand that's not happening. My future is as a screenwriter."

The silent conversation going on between her parents was quite entertaining, even if she had no idea what they were saying. Her parents had been together so long they could basically communicate their thoughts and feelings with a raised eyebrow or pursed lip.

"Well that's wonderful, darling." Her dad rose from his chair and crossed the short distance to give her a quick hug. "Where are you headed for your research trip?"

"Virginia. There's a Navy SEAL base there."

"Virginia?" Her mom asked. "Why not go to San Diego. It's closer."

And close enough for you to lure me back to L.A. on some pretext when you find the next victim you want me to marry.

No way would she tell her mother that, no matter how annoying she was being. Despite Bettina's attempts to not listen to her daughter, Amberley had no doubt her mother loved her in her own unique way.

"True, but I don't know anyone in San Diego. I know someone in Virginia who's in the Navy and has been helping me with any questions I've had. Now I want to go see him and immerse myself into how a Navy SEAL lives and the job he does. Draw those experiences into my script." The more she talked the more feasible and believable it sounded.

"That's a good idea, sweetheart," her father commented from his position back in his chair.

"Yes, why don't we make it a girls trip. It'll be fun to be just the two of us." Bettina smiled a satisfied glint entering her eyes, as if the plans were all finalized and didn't require further instruction. It was a look Amberley was familiar with.

"Geez, Mom, no. No girls trip. I don't need you to come with me. I'm a grown woman. I live by myself. I'll be fine. Besides I won't be among strangers. I'll be with Thomas Grant. He'll be helping me and I'll be staying with him." Mentally crossing her fingers that Tom would be willing to help her, not to mention let her stay with him.

Shit, what if he lived on base and didn't have room for her? She brushed the thought away. If she had to, she'd stay in a hotel. Her parents didn't need to know that.

"Thomas Grant? Isn't he the brother of that Jenny girl?"

Amberley controlled the urge to roll her eyes. Her mom hadn't really appreciated the likes of Jenny and her brother Thomas in Amberley's life. What purpose did it serve to have people in your life who couldn't help your career, her mom had prattled to her over and over. But she'd been determined to have a sort of normal life. As normal as she could get with who her parents and grandparents were. But for a short while she had and it had been a wonderful time of her life.

"Yes, Mom, Thomas is Jenny's brother and you know he serves his country. I don't like that you talk down about him. He puts his life on the line time and again so you can drive around in your Bentley and drink it up with your fake friends at the Beverly Hills Hotel. And," she paused going in for the kill. "He's my boyfriend."

CHAPTER TWO

Thomas 'Red' Grant laughed at something Joker said while pulling out his phone which had vibrated with an incoming message.

He looked down and saw Amberley's name in the little rectangular box on his home screen. Every time he saw her name, his heart rate kicked up a notch and this time was no different. If the guys knew she was sending him a message they'd give him a hard time. They already did whenever he answered one of her texts.

No matter how many times he told them he and Amberley were just friends, they didn't believe him. If the truth be told, he kept saying it in an attempt to convince himself. She was his little sister's best friend, and there was the unwritten rule that you didn't tap your sister's friends, no matter how sexy and attractive they were. The flirty texts didn't help.

Before he could unlock his phone the device rang. Once again Amberley's name popped up. Why was she calling? She never called. Their dealings had always been via text message.

Anxiety that something had happened to Jenny and her husband had him swiping to accept the call quicker than a jackrabbit.

"Amberley, it's Red, what's up?"

"Red? Thomas is that you?"

Tom walked away from the guys when he noted that conversation had stopped the second he'd mentioned Amberley's name. Yeah, he'd be getting twenty questions when he finished with the call.

"Sorry, yeah, Amberley, it's me, Tom. Red is my nickname."

"Oh, that's right. I forgot you guys give yourselves nicknames. I'll have to make a note of that in my script. Umm, so listen." Amberley paused, the silence lengthening. Even though the anxiety that something had happened to Jenny had partially faded, he still remained poised to spring into action if needed. "I hope you're not too busy, it's just that I'm at Norfolk International airport. Do you think you can come and get me?"

Whatever he'd been expecting, for Amberley to say she was at the local airport, wasn't it. "What? You're here? Why? Has something happened to Jenny?" Voicing his earlier thought.

The second he finished talking, he realized how ridiculous that sounded. Amberley wouldn't fly out to see him if Jenny was badly hurt. It would be far quicker to relay the bad news via a phone call. And the phone call would come from his parents not his sister's best friend.

"No. No. Jenny and Darren are fine. But, well, I needed some space and so here I am."

Again there was a slight hesitation in her words. What was up with that? "Are you okay? Are you the one in trouble?"

She laughed, but again it sounded strained to his ears. "No, not really. And why is someone in trouble or danger your immediate go to?

"Occupational hazard, Ambs. But you said *not really* when I asked so what's going on?"

"Well if you want to be technical I guess you could call annoying my parents being in trouble."

Tom recalled her parents. Who didn't know Bettina and John Price. You'd have to live under a rock not to recognize their names. The guys on the team didn't know that Amberley was their daughter. If they did, the hell they'd give him would be tripled.

As it was, being the only single guy on the team now had him feeling like a third wheel on some occasions.

"Well I can't help you with your parents, but can help you out with a ride. Give me twenty minutes and I'll be there."

"Thanks, Tom, it means a lot." Her voiced lowered and his body reacted to her sultry tones, especially hearing her call him by the shortened version of his name. She'd only ever called him Thomas.

"Not an issue. I'm always here to help Jenny's friends." And friend was all she could be, no matter how much he was attracted to her.

Disconnecting the call he strode over to where Cowboy and Faith stood by the grill.

"I've got to go. Sorry about missing lunch." Tom walked away without giving them a chance to respond. It was rude, but the need to get to Amberley wasn't something he could ignore.

He'd almost made his escape when Robot, his team lead, came over to him. "Red, everything okay?"

"Yeah, it's nothing. My sister's friend called. She's at Norfolk Airport and needs a ride. I'm going to get her."

"Is everything okay? Is she in trouble?"

Funny, how his team lead asked the same questions he'd asked Amberley. As he'd told her—occupational hazard. "Nah, she's fine. I'll see you tomorrow at PT."

Making his escape, he headed toward his SUV, glad he wasn't boxed in and would have to get the other guys to move their cars. Tomorrow would be soon enough to answer all their questions. At least by then he'd have some sort of idea why Amberley was escaping her parents.

Gunning the engine, he took off in the direction of the airport, his thoughts drifting to the woman he was about to pick up and her star-studded family. Bettina Price had never been happy with Amberley and Jennifer's friendship. He had to admit when Jenny had first introduced him to Amberley he'd been a little star struck. The fact his little sister was acting cooler than he was, hadn't been lost on him. He'd been fifteen and a mass of raging teenage hormones and there was a TV star in his house.

Over time she'd become just Amberley, his sister's best friend and not Amberley the star. It had been hard to give off an *I don't give a shit about you* attitude around her. It was the exact opposite—he'd wanted more than anything to kiss her and maybe more. Jenny had picked up on his crush and had told him all about the *best friends code*—no hitting on friends—a code he'd never heard before.

Jenny had gone back on her word and started

seeing one of his friends, Darren. By the time he'd found out he'd moved on from his crush, and was dating the head cheerleader through junior and senior year of high school. After graduation they probably had the most amicable break-up ever. He had no regrets dating Joanna, but he couldn't deny every time he saw Amberley he always wondered *what if*.

Was this now his what if time?

Tom shook that thought out of his head as he slid into a parking spot. Picking up his phone he sent Amberley a text.

I'M HERE. WHERE ARE YOU?

His phone beeped pretty much straight away.

BAGGAGE CLAIM. FIGURED THIS WAS AS GOOD AS PLACE AS ANY TO WAIT.

At least she wasn't outside. There wasn't a lot of press hanging around the airport, not many celebrities flew into Norfolk, but someone could've recognized her, snapped a picture of her and put it all over social media. Her show may have ended, but who her parents were would never change so she still had enough star power for a photo to go viral.

Fuck, it must suck to live life like that.

I'LL BE THERE IN FIVE

Pocketing his phone he walked into the airport, immediately scanning the area, noting the people with backpacks, the child crying and clinging to its mother's leg. Everyone seemed to be going about their business like normal, but that never meant anything. Things could change in a heartbeat. He'd been on enough missions to see how quickly a situation could go from normal to chaotic.

Striding through the terminal he located the baggage claim area and headed down there. The space was packed as it looked like a couple of planes had landed at the same time. Finding Amberley would be a challenge seeing as he didn't know if she wore a disguise. It wouldn't surprise him if she did.

"Thomas!"

He turned in the direction of his name and his breath caught. Amberley was walking toward him, a big smile on her face, rolling a suitcase next to her. She looked even more beautiful since the last time he saw her at his sister's wedding.

Her maid of honor dress had clung to her body in all the right places. The hardest thing he had to do was walk away that night, but, he'd gotten a call for a mission and had to miss most of the reception. Today she had on a pair of skinny jeans and, was that?

He narrowed his eyes and then threw his head back and laughed—she had an Iron Man t-shirt on.

"Nice t-shirt. Glad you came to your senses."

"I wouldn't go that far. But, I could be persuaded. Or," she paused, looking up at him from beneath her eyelashes. "I could change your mind."

Before he had a chance to comprehend her flirty look, her arms were around his neck and her body pressed into his. Her flowery scent wafted around him and reminded him of the roses growing in his mother's front yard. Reflexively his arms circled her waist. With their bodies pressed close together, it was impossible not to feel the shudder ripple through her body.

"Really? How?"

She smiled and touched his face. "Maybe like this."

A second later her lips were glued to his. Shock held him as immobile as a statue.

Amberley Price was kissing him.

The teenage boy he'd once been reveled in the sensation. The adult man he was now reacted like any hot-blooded male would when a gorgeous woman kissed him. He shifted the angle of his head and deepened the kiss. His dick went hard against the zipper of his jeans. Her fingers dug into his back and scrunched up the loose sweater he wore.

They were in the middle of the airport creating a scene. He should pull back. Put some distance between them, but he'd been wanting this moment for so long that he planned to savor and memorize it.

Who knew when this would happen again?

The need to breathe had them separating, both their chests heaving in sync. As if it sunk in at what she'd done, Amberley stepped out of his hold, a pink hue highlighting her cheeks. He wasn't sure if it was from their kisses or embarrassment.

Tom cleared his throat and spied her bag sitting on the ground beside her. "Right, that's a different form of persuasion. But, um, yeah, we should go." He grabbed the handle and headed back in the direction he came, hoping Amberley followed.

As he passed through the throng of people he observed the speculative looks on their faces. Yeah, he and Amberley had given a pretty good display of public affection right then.

God, he hoped no one recognized Amberley and snapped a photo of them together. As a SEAL it was imperative that he was discrete when in public. The last thing he or the team needed was his face splashed across the gossip pages of every internet site.

He couldn't believe he'd been so irresponsible. He and Amberley were from completely different worlds. Worlds that didn't belong together. Kissing Amberley couldn't ever happen again.

Amberley hurried to keep up with Thomas. She was tall but for every step she took, he took two.

What the hell had she been thinking to just kiss him like that?

She never indulged in PDA's, and there'd been plenty of times some of her *dates* wanted to give the impression they were more than a photo opportunity set up by their respective agents. No one had come up to her while she'd waited for him, but she'd seen people give her a second look when they walked past.

What if one of them had taken a photo of her and Tom kissing?

Anyone could upload a picture of stars these days. There were so many social media sites that people were on all the time. She'd avoided social media as much as possible. She worked hard at keeping a low profile, even with her high profile parents.

All she could hope for was that her kiss with Thomas would not be the next hour's lead news story.

The warm sun hit her face as she walked outside and she was glad she still had her sunglasses on. A slight breeze ruffled her hair and she dug into her tote to pull out a hat and popped it on. One thing her mother always made sure she carried—a hat and sunglasses, because *you never know when you will need it Amberley*. For once her mother was right.

Her lips still tingled from their contact with Thomas. How many nights had Amberley lay on the twin bed in Jenny's room, imaging her friend's big brother kissing her? Too many to count.

Amberley had loved being around Jenny and her family. After their initial shock and awe that their daughter had a teenage TV star as a friend, they'd begun to treat her like a normal girl and she'd loved it. At the Grant's house she could have all the food her mother forbade her from having. It had been freeing and when Thomas had graduated and gone off to basic training with the Navy, she'd cried in her pillow that she never had the courage to tell him she liked him.

Well here she was following him, and about to spend time with him. Only he didn't know that little tidbit yet. She'd cross that bridge when he asked her which hotel she was staying at.

He stopped by a silver SUV, not the type of car she expected a single guy to drive. It looked more like a family car. Then again, he was part of a team, it made sense to have a big car. If the rest of the team were as tall and muscular as Thomas, squeezing into a muscle car would be a challenge. Not to mention a sight to see. Maybe she could write that into the script. It would make for a fun scene and bring some lightness to the movie.

Yes, she liked that idea a lot. Quickly she pulled out her tablet and opened up her One Note document to make some notes.

"What are you doing?" He asked and she jumped, he had moved to stand beside her.

She looked up at him, her gaze landing on the lips she'd locked with not ten minutes ago. "Umm. I, umm." *Get a grip, girl*, she admonished herself. "I had an idea for a scene for the movie I'm writing and I wanted to get it down before I forgot it."

He reached around her, his warmth enveloping her and she steeled her spine from leaning back into him. "Well how about you do it in the car. The parking lot is not the safest place to be loitering around taking notes on a device that could be snatched out of your hand." He pulled the door open.

How long had it been that someone other than a driver had opened the door for her? The dates she'd been on in the past not one of the guys had opened the door for her. But it seemed natural that Thomas would do it.

"Thanks," she murmured as she ducked under his arm and got into the car.

The leather seat was cool after the warmth from the sun. The interior was spotless. Had he just had the car detailed or did he always keep it this clean? Probably the latter. She couldn't imagine that Thomas would be a slob with his car.

The first time she'd snuck a look into his room she'd been surprised by how neat it was. The bed was made, not precisely, but still made. No clothes laid over the back of his desk chair or strewn on the floor. His desk had books piled up neatly in one corner. She imagined if she'd opened his closet all his clothes would be lined up in an orderly row. When she'd asked Jenny about it, her friend had laughed and said Thomas liked a clean space. Jenny, on the other hand, well her room had looked lived in and Amberley had loved it.

Amberley's own room had been as neat as Thomas's, whereas Thomas's room held books and trophies and had a lived in feel, even as clean as it was. Her room always seemed sterile, as if, like her, constantly on display. She'd never been able to relax for fear her mother would come in and scold her for putting a crease in the bed cover.

"Where do I need to take you?" Thomas asked, pulling her from her thoughts.

Taking a deep breath, she smiled at him. "Your place?"

"What?"

Amberley was glad they were still in the parking lot and not out on the road with the way Thomas looked at her as if she'd sprouted another head. She reached over the console and placed her hand on his forearm, the muscles bunched beneath her touch.

"Please, Tom. I know it's out of the blue but if the roles were reversed you know I'd let you stay at my place without question. And I know Jenny would be happier knowing that I was with you and not in some hotel." A little white lie but she wasn't above pulling out the big guns if she had to, and mentioning Thomas's little sister was a sure fire way to get him to agree with her.

His fingers clenched around the steering wheel and with her hand still on his arm, she felt the muscles contracting.

God, what would he look like naked?

Would he have a six-pack? Duh, of course he would, the guy probably worked out every day. Had to, no doubt, with his job.

His job.

That was another thing she could use to persuade him to let her stay with him.

"You know how I texted you questions about the things you do?"

"Yeah. What about it?" He answered cautiously.

While he'd been forthcoming with information, he'd also been pretty vague and cagey when she tried to get specifics out of him. He'd told her that for his and his team's safety, not to mention the well-being of the people they'd rescued, he couldn't go into the nitty gritty of his job. She respected that, even though she'd been disappointed at the same time.

"Well I'm writing the screenplay for a major action and adventure movie. I've come out here to, not only escape my parents." She'd been honest about that, she had needed space from her mom's interference. "But also to see if I can get some inside information about what you do and how you do things on a mission. I want to give the movie as much of an authentic feel as I can."

Instead of answering he shook her hand off, started the car and pulled out of the bay. Amberley tried not to feel disconcerted with the way he'd removed her grip, like she was a pesky fly. And especially after the hot kiss they'd just shared.

Once they'd cleared the parking garage and were on the road, he spoke. "Okay, well in answer to your first question, yes you can come and stay with me. It's not much but I do happen to have a spare room."

"Thank you, I appreciate it. I promise I won't get in your way."

"Yeah, well that remains to be seen." He chuckled and the sound reverberated down her spine. He'd always had that effect on her. It had taken everything in her when she was a teenager not to try and sneak a kiss or two from him when Jenny wasn't looking.

Unfortunately, he'd always put up barriers whenever she tried to get close to him, and then he'd had a girlfriend his final two years of high school. Eventually Jenny had spilled that she'd told him to stay away from Amberley. That little bit of information had hurt her. Why would her best friend do that to her? Especially after she'd hooked up with one of Thomas's friends. But by then Thomas was dating Joanna so there was no way anything could have happened between them.

Well they weren't teenagers now. Jenny and Darren were married and they were nowhere near to see what she and Thomas did.

"As for your second request, I'm not sure if you'll be granted access on base. There's a reason we keep our tactics on the downlow. Not only are our missions classified, we don't want the enemy to know what we do. We're so successful on our missions because of the element of surprise."

"Oh, right. Damn." A stab of disappointed flowed

through her at not being able to watch Thomas's team as they trained.

"I'll try and helps as much as I can, Ambs. I'll even talk to Robot and see what I can do."

"Robot? Is that like a machine you punch things into or something." Amberley pictured a structure of shiny metal and flashing lights, with a keyboard and a built-in printer.

"He's a real person not a machine. Brendan is his name and he's my team lead. Robot is his nickname."

"Do all of you guys have nicknames?" She recalled that when he answered her call he'd called himself *Red*.

"Yeah we do."

"And yours is Red?"

It was almost comical the way he whipped his eyes off the road and looked at her. "How do you know that?"

She shrugged, surprised he'd forgotten he'd told her. "You answered my call, and identified yourself as *Red*, and then you told me it was your nickname, remember?

"Right, I did."

"Your team leader has a cool nickname."

"Team Lead."

"What?" Confusion filled her. Had she missed part of the conversation? She didn't think she had.

"Robot is a team lead, not team leader. You should make a note of that as well."

"Right, will do. So how did you get your nickname? Did you tell the guys what to call you?"

Thomas chuckled. "No we don't pick our own nicknames. If we did we'd all have something cooler than Red, Italy, or Robot."

She cocked her head to the side. "Well I've already said Robot's name is cool. The others all sound reasonable too. And intriguing. Go on tell me how you got yours." She cajoled and batted her eyelashes at him. Not that he saw her do that because his focus was on the road. She did, however, note that his fingers flexed a little tighter around the steering wheel.

"It's not very exciting but I turned up at BUD/s training badly sunburned. One of the guys training us pointed and yelled at me, *Red, move your slow ass*. By the end of the drill everyone else was calling me Red and that was it. That's how I got my name."

Amberley laughed, she could totally visualize it in her mind. During her research she'd found out about the brutal training course they weren't through to become a SEAL. "Oh that's priceless. And everyone gets their nicknames at BUD/s training?"

"Not always, some guys already come with nicknames. The guys all have their own stories for how they got their names."

Interesting and something she definitely would include when it came to writing her script. Maybe she could talk to the rest of his team to find out how they all got their nicknames. Even though it had been a spur of the moment decision, she was really glad that she decided to visit Thomas. Although keeping her hands to herself was going to be harder now.

CHAPTER THREE

What the hell was he thinking agreeing to let Amberley stay at his house? Not to mention telling her how he got his nickname. Not that he was ashamed of his nickname, well maybe a little embarrassed, but he did his job and that was all that mattered. Resisting Amberley was going to be impossible now. Especially after the kiss she'd laid on him when he greeted her at the airport.

What was with that anyway? Never before had she shown any indication that she was into him. If she had he wasn't sure what he would've done. It had to mean nothing. Although it didn't feel like nothing.

"Hey Tom, do you have any coke? I can only see diet coke in the fridge" Amberley strolled into the living room of his apartment. She'd had a shower not long after they'd arrived at his place. She claimed she wanted to wash off the remnants of travelling in a tin can breathing recycled air of the occupants. Now she wore a long flowing dress that hinted at luscious curves begging for him to explore. He kind of missed the Iron Man shirt, but she looked cool, calm and as sexy as sin. And he was calling on all his training to resist kissing her again.

While she'd been showering he'd run out to the store and picked up a few groceries. Things he thought she might like, including diet coke.

"Don't all Hollywood people like diet stuff? You know, they want a skinny latte or soy milk Frappuccino."

Amberley busted out laughing and he enjoyed the sweet sound of it. "Thomas Grant you've been watching too many TV shows." She came over and sat next to him on the couch. A waft of fresh coconut floated around him. He breathed in, and the scent reminded him of sun, sand and days at the beach where people smeared coconut oil over their skin in an attempt to get the perfect tan.

It wouldn't take much to imagine him rubbing oil over Amberley's half naked body. She'd looked amazing in a bikini as a teenager and he had no doubt as an adult, she'd look even better.

His dick twitched against his jeans and he jumped

up from the couch. The last thing Amberley needed to see was how she affected him. That was a secret he'd rather keep to himself. Kiss or not, he wasn't going to cross the line and wreck the friendship they had. "I'll, um, go to the store and get you some coke. I won't be long."

Again the scent of coconut assailed him and he closed his eyes, willing is body to settle the hell down. He tensed when her hand landed on his shoulder.

"It's okay. I don't mind diet coke, I just prefer the real stuff. No need to go out and make another trip. You're already going above and beyond for me when I pulled this surprise on you." She pointed back to the couch. "Why don't we sit and we can talk more about some of the things I need for my script. I'm really interested to know about the nickname thing, like how the rest of the guys on your team got theirs. I wanted to ask you more in the car, but that guy cut us off and I didn't want to distract you so I didn't say anything."

Tom blew out a breath. He'd only been around her for less than two hours and already he was strung tighter than a piano wire. The reason he'd run out to the store was because he didn't want to think about a naked Amberley in his shower. Thank fuck his apartment had two bathrooms along with the two bedrooms. Sharing a bathroom with Amberley would be hell on wheels.

Hopefully her visit wasn't going to be long. Geez, he was a Navy SEAL, he'd been trained to deal with stressful situations, and while this wasn't like any of the situations he and his team went into, he could use some of those techniques to get him through Amberley's visit. All he had to remember was she came from a completely different world than him and the two could never mesh together.

"Sure, that's fine. Let me grab a drink and then we can talk."

He escaped into the kitchen and opened the refrigerator, the cool air doing nothing to ease the fire of desire simmering within him.

Tom grabbed a can of diet coke and his hand hovered over the green glass bottle of his favorite brew. Instead of grabbing it he withdrew a bottle of water. With Amberley around he needed a clear head. For the duration of her visit his alcohol consumption was going to be kept to a minimum.

He paused outside the living room when he heard Amberley talking. It sounded like she was on a call and he didn't want to interrupt if it was private. But his ears pricked up when he heard his name.

"Yeah, mom, Thomas got me from the airport. I'm at his place now."

There was a pause where he imagined her mother was talking. Nothing Bettina said would shock to him. Amberley's mom was probably chastising her for staying with a man well below her standing in life, instead of the presidential suite at a five star hotel as befitting her star status. Not that she'd been a star for years, but her parents were still revered in Hollywood.

"I told you mom, Thomas and I are together now. You're just going to have to accept it. He makes me happy."

What the actual fuck?

Did Amberley just tell her mother that they were an item? It sounded pretty clear to him, but if they were together it was certainly news to him. Although it would explain the kiss.

He walked into the room as Amberley turned around, her eyes widened in surprise. Her neck and face reddened when it dawned on her that he'd overhead the last part of her conversation.

"I've got to go, Mom. I'll call you later." She pulled the phone away from her ear and tossed it on the couch. "Before you get mad, I can explain."

Tom placed the drinks on the table and crossed his arms over his chest. "I hope so, because what I heard was very interesting. And a total surprise, *honey*."

O*h shit.*

Why had she not looked around before she blurted that out to her mom? Simple, her mom had been lecturing her, again, about taking off and leaving a perfectly good man like Rob Gregor behind. Convincing mom that she and Thomas were an item was a much better option, than breaking Rob's confidence about his sexual preferences.

"You'll laugh when I explain it all to you." She started and fiddled with the fabric of her long dress.

"I'm sure it's quite the story," he drawled. "But I expect the truth Amberley and not some screenplay you're writing. If I think you're lying our deal is off and you'll be staying at a hotel instead of here."

She sucked in a breath. Okay, she'd expected a little pushback, but she never thought he'd renege on their deal. She needed his help.

"I would never lie to you, Tom."

"Yet you lied to your mom. How do I know you won't lie to me?" he asked as he sat on the couch.

Damn, he had a point. Then again he had no idea the lengths her mother had gone to over the last few months. How desperate she was to be able to do her own thing and not what her mom deemed the best for her.

Amberley walked over to where he sat and plopped down next to him. Holding her breath a beat to see if he would get up and put some space between them. When he remained where he was, she relaxed a fraction. Okay maybe this wouldn't be so bad. "I wouldn't lie to you because you're my friend."

"I suppose I should be flattered. But it doesn't explain why you lied to your mom. I'm pretty sure she'll be happy to find out we're not together. I'm not exactly her first choice for you. However, I do think she'd be upset that you lied to her."

The point he made was valid. Mom would for sure experience mixed emotions—happy that she and Tom weren't together, but not happy about her lying. Secretly, though, Amberley wanted her lie to be true. She hoped that by the end of her stay she and Tom were a couple. Then her mom wouldn't have to know she'd fudged the truth a little.

"If you understood what I've been through the last few months, I think you won't be so angry. Will you let me explain before you say anything else, please?" She paused, reaching over to grab the can of soda from the table. Popping the top she took a swallow as she waited for his answer.

"Fine. I'll listen and not interrupt." Like her he grabbed his drink and gulped some down. The way his throat moved up and down was mesmerizing.

Shaking her head she took another drink and then placed the can back on the table.

Lacing her fingers together she sat straight and gazed at the blank flat screen television hanging on the wall opposite from where they were sitting. "Mom has always wanted me to go back into acting. She's constantly shoving movie and television scripts under my nose. Telling me I'd be perfect for this part or that part. Bettina Price can't understand why the prodigy of two Hollywood A-List actors doesn't want to have her name in lights. Or her face on the big screen in every movie theatre in the United States.

"She won't accept that's not how I want to live my life. Yes, I enjoyed being on the sitcom when I was younger, but now my passion is in creating words. I want to see and hear people acting out what I write. Bring the vision in my mind to life on the screen, either movie or television. But she doesn't see that. She's sees it as a waste of my time. There's no money in screenwriting in her mind. I'd be better off working in front of the camera. That's where the money is."

Amberley jumped when an arm banded around her shoulder and she found herself being tugged down against a warm male chest. She breathed out and relaxed against Thomas's side, placing a hand on his rock hard abs before continuing. "Mom is determined that not only should I go back to acting, but the time has come for me to marry. She's been inviting suitable guys over to dinner for weeks. All of them are falling all over themselves to impress Mom and Dad with witty comments and agreeing with everything they say. All of them also tried to hit on me in some way or another. One guy, Simon, was so annoying that I ended up having to threaten him with a restraining order before he took the hint and left me alone." Thomas's muscles tensed beneath her chin and she noted his reaction and popped it to the back of her mind so she could examine it later. "In the end I needed to get away. It's true I've asked you questions about what you guys do and you've helped me, but this script is a huge stepping stone in my career. I want to make it as authentic as possible so when the last dinner didn't pan out like Mom hoped, and never would because the guy totally wasn't into me and I wasn't into him, I blurted out that I was coming to see you and that we were in a relationship."

Remembering how she'd dropped that bomb on her parents and walked out on them still had the ability to make her cringe. Her mom's demands for an explanation ringing loudly in her ears as she escaped to her house down the road from her parent's compound. Sometimes she was still like the impetuous character she'd played on the sitcom. Maybe that was why she'd acted the part so well, she was really playing herself.

It had taken some careful planning and stealth moves, but she'd managed to leave without her mom knocking on her door demanding answers. Although doing that would go against everything in Bettina's life. People came to her, she didn't go to them, her daughter included.

Thomas's fingers played with her hair and she closed her eyes, enjoying the sensation. At least he hadn't pushed her away. "Seems like she's still not onboard with our *relationship* from the little I could make out from your conversation with her."

Amberley reached over and played with the buttons on his shirt. "Yeah, I don't understand what her issue is. Your job is one to be admired not ridiculed. You'd think she'd be happy that I was happy."

Beneath her chin his chest lifted and dropped as he took in a deep breath. "But it's all a lie, Ambs, we're not a couple. Never have been."

Never will be.

The words weren't spoken out loud, but they hung in the air between them and she hated it.

She wouldn't mind being in relationship with Thomas, it was why the lie had tripped off her tongue so easily. All through that dinner with Rob he'd been on her mind. They hadn't seen each other since Jenny's wedding. Had only just recently started talking again. Sporadic as it was, it had still been communication between them. Their last text conversation had been flirtier than anything they'd ever exchanged.

"I know. It was stupid of me to put you in this situation. If you want to take me to a hotel I'll understand. I shouldn't have used you like this."

His lips brushed against her temple and she sighed, closing her eyes at the brief contact. It wouldn't be a hardship to lay in his arms like this on the couch night after night. Her life may have been made up of living in a large guesthouse on a thirty-acre property, not having to worry about watching her pennies and being able to buy whatever she wanted. Although the lure of being able to have everything she'd wanted had died off pretty quickly. In the end she liked a simple life. Liked the quas-anonymity she lived with now.

Unlike her parents, she didn't thrive with constantly being in the spotlight.

A finger hooked under her chin, lifting it so that she looked deep into Thomas's smooth brown eyes. "I'm not sending you away, Ambs. You can stay here for as long as you need."

Two sentences.

That's all it took for the worry about him kicking her out to leave and a different kind of tension to build up between them. Her gaze dropped to his lips and she recalled the feel of them against hers from the kiss they'd shared at the airport. Firm, yet soft. Her mouth dried imagining another taste. Imagining Thomas lowering her back to the couch and him leaning over her before he captured her lips again.

Her tongue darted out and swiped across her dry lips. A split second later her fantasy came to life, as though Thomas had reached into her mind and plucked it out. Her back was on the soft cushions of his couch, and his face was inches from hers.

"This could be a huge mistake, but I don't care," he muttered before he closed the gap and kissed her. The hair on her arms rose as gooseflesh rippled over her skin. Her fingers gripped his biceps as he lowered himself on top of her. She relished having him this close.

For so long she'd wanted to be in his arms. Have his lips on her and nothing she'd conjured up in her mind could compare with the reality of it. His body aligned with hers perfectly, like they were made for each other. Her nipples peaked against her bra and she rubbed her chest against his muscular one. His hips jerked against hers and she couldn't miss how much the kiss was affecting him. His hard length rested at the perfect spot between her legs.

What would it be like to be naked like this? Knowing that with one thrust he would be buried deep inside her?

A shaft of desire arrowed through her, wetting her already damp panties. Her hands moved to the waistband of his jeans, grabbing at his shirt, pushing it up until she could trail her fingers across the small strip of flesh she'd exposed.

Thomas broke the kiss far too soon for her liking. One second she was caressing his back, the next she was by herself on the couch and he was standing on the opposite side of the room.

Amberley sat up and smoothed down her dress. She resisted the urge to press her fingers against her lips, imprinting the kiss into them. "Are you okay?"

He glanced at her, his face impassive. The lips that only seconds ago were locked with hers, now resembled a thin line. His shirt was still untucked and his hair was ruffled, giving him the just out of bed look. It suited him, but mentioning that to him wouldn't be wise.

"Yeah." He scrubbed his hands through his hair, messing it even more, before they fell to his side. "Are you hungry? It's getting late."

Okay, so not what she expected him to say but

now that she thought about it, she was famished. Her last meal had been a long time ago and she hadn't wanted to risk eating anything on the flight over. Amberley was sure the sandwiches the airlines supplied were perfectly fine, she just never trusted airline food.

"Umm yeah, that would be great. What do you have in mind?" Wow how had they gone from steaming hot kisses on the couch to polite, formal conversation about food?

"If I remember, you like pizza. There's a great pizza place not far from here, they deliver."

"Pizza sounds fine."

"Good. Great. I'll go order it."

He was out of the room before she could say anything else. She flopped against the back of the couch again.

Well this was going to be fun.

CHAPTER FOUR

Tom disconnected the call to the pizza joint and tossed his phone on the kitchen counter. He closed his eyes and visions of the kiss he shared with Amberley played across his eyelids.

What the hell had he been thinking kissing her again?

Simple fact, he wasn't. He'd listened to her story, trying hard to ignore the stab of jealousy in his gut when she talked about the guys her mother had tried to set her up with. He hadn't liked hearing about the guy who wouldn't leave her alone. If the asshole tried anything while he was around, he'd regret it.

What the hell?

He needed to stop thinking that way. They weren't in a relationship. Once Amberley went back to L.A. her mother would continue with her search for Amberley's perfect husband.

Perfect husband.

Whoever it ended up being, they would probably have the right family connections. Overflowing bank accounts and didn't put their life on the line every day of their life. He didn't want that life. He wanted the one he had and he was damn proud of what he did. But all the guys were settling down and seeing them so happy had him wondering if he would ever be as lucky as them.

You've got Amberley here. You had her in your arms. A place she seemed happy being.

One thing he didn't have was any claim over Amberley. She came from Hollywood royalty. There was no chance for them. Besides, she was Jenny's best friend.

Why the fuck did that matter?

Exactly, why did it matter? Was there really an unwritten rule that you couldn't hook up with your sister's best friend? Sure, Jenny had told him to keep his hands off her friend and he had. Why was he still clinging to her wishes when his sister had gone ahead and broken it anyway fucking years ago by hooking up with his friend?

Because that was who he was. He'd made a promise to his sister. Sure the promise had been when he'd been a teenager, and shouldn't still be an issue now. It shouldn't hold him back from going after what he wanted. Jenny certainly hadn't let it. Truthfully, he was the only one who was having issues. Did Amberley even know about the Jenny's command to him? Had his sister mentioned it to her at all. Not that it mattered in the grand scheme of things.

"Tom, did you order the pizza?"

He turned and plastered a smile on his face, keeping his gaze averted from her luscious lips. Her dress wasn't the sexiest thing in the world, but fuck did it turn him on. Underneath the fabric were curves he'd dream about tonight, without a doubt.

"Yeah. Should be here in about forty minutes."

As she gazed around the room, and fidgeted with the material of her dress, he could tell she was as rattled as he was by the kiss.

What would she do if he threw caution to the wind and swept her up in his arms and strode to his room? If he consumed her body and made her his. After the way she kissed him back, touched him back, he didn't think she would object to it.

A second later her eyes lifted and connected with his. Desire blazed in them, turning the irises from dark green to bright emerald. His dick immediately responded, going hard again.

"Fuck it," he muttered and crossed the room in two strides. "I'm done playing it safe."

He cupped the back of her head and slipped an arm around her waist, pulling her tight against him. Her arms immediately looped his neck and she melted into him. Their lips met and everything dissolved from his mind except the woman in his arms.

Her mouth opened beneath his and he thrust his tongue in, telling her exactly what he wanted to do to her. The way she moaned beneath his onslaught left no doubt in his mind she was on board with what he wanted to do.

Gripping her beneath her ass he lifted her and she wound her legs around his hips, bringing her hot heat in line with his throbbing dick. She ground her hips and he almost came in his pants, something he hadn't done since he was thirteen.

The need to be inside Amberley pushed all sensible thoughts to the side. In this moment all he wanted was to feel her inner muscles clench around him as he thrust into her. He should take her to his bedroom, lay her out and worship her body. But his desire for her consumed him and he didn't think he'd make it.

He walked them until Amberley's back connected with the wall. Anchoring her against it, he bunched up her long dress until he found her panties. He slipped a finger beneath the elastic and stroked her slick folds.

If possible her moans got louder with every pass he made.

"God, you're so wet. I want to taste you but I need inside you right now."

"Do it, Tom. Take me." Her hands were frantically trying to get to his jeans.

As much as he didn't want to, he set her feet on the ground while he reached into his back pocket and pulled out his wallet to get the condom he always carried with him. Amberley leaned forward and kissed his neck, causing his fingers to slacken and he nearly dropped the foil packet.

His lips chased hers until they were connected again. At least if he was in control of her mouth he wouldn't lose the condom—delaying the moment when he could possess her fully.

One handed he undid his jeans and shoved them and his boxers down. He broke the contact with Amberley's mouth so he could rip open the condom. Once he sheathed himself, he gathered up her dress again and lifted it. Amberley raised her arms and he pulled it over her head, tossing the soft fabric over his shoulder.

All his teenage dreams hadn't prepared him for

the vision leaning against the wall. Standing in only a scrap of white lace, Tom took his fill of her. Her breasts were beautiful mounds of flesh, and her nipples puckered under his scrutiny.

There was so much he wanted to do to her. Make her orgasm from just playing with her breasts. Hear her screams of delight as he made her come from eating her out. Most of all he wanted to have her wet heat surround his cock as he sent her into oblivion.

His dick jerked, clearly agreeing with the last scenario.

"You're so beautiful, Ambs. So many places I want to taste and explore, but I need to be inside you now." He closed the distance between them and, once again, lifted her so she could wind her legs around him.

Holding her at the perfect angle, he guided himself to her entrance, teasing her with his tip.

"Geez, Tom, do it. Stop teasing. I want you. I've wanted you for so long."

He chuckled against her neck, nibbling at her tender skin as he slowly slid into her. Tom wanted to savior their first time together. This moment of connection was a long time in the making, and from her declaration, it wasn't one-sided.

It seemed Amberley wanted him as much as he wanted her. If he'd known that all those years ago, he might have acted on it. For so long he thought Amberley was ambivalent toward him. And why wouldn't she be? He had nothing to offer her. He still didn't, not in comparison to the guys her mom no doubt paraded in front of her.

But what he could, and would do, was love her until she couldn't stand. With one last thrust he seated himself deeply in her. A shudder rippled through him and an answering one swept through Amberley.

"Oh, God, you feel so good," she arched herself into him, brushing her luscious breasts against his chest.

That was all he needed, he started to move then. Sliding out before thrusting back in. Her fingernails dug into his back and he relished the sting of the contact.

He couldn't wait until he got her in his bed, where he could lick, suck and nibble his way down her body. Taste her sweet juices on his tongue. Hear her scream out his name as her orgasm ripped through her body.

All those thoughts of what he wanted to do, increased his desire to make her come right now. She chanted his name in his ear and her inner muscles greedily grabbed at his cock every time he slid out.

He couldn't last much longer, but he wanted to make sure Amberley reached her release before him.

Adjusting his hold he angled deeper in her on the next thrust and a scream rent the air as her body shuddered around him in release. He hung on to her tight as he stroked into her one last time before his own climax hit him. He held her close until his body stopped shaking.

Tom dropped his head to her shoulder, licking at her skin, tasting the faint saltiness of it. "Are you okay?" he whispered.

Her arms tightened around him and another shudder rippled through her. "More than okay. That was everything and more."

Before he could respond she lifted his head and captured his lips with her own. Inside her his cock jumped a little.

Yeah, it wouldn't be long before he was ready for round two.

Amberley pulled her lips from his when she felt the movement of Tom's dick inside of her. "Are you serious?"

He chuckled and, because of their connection, it flowed through her. "What can I say. You're very tempting."

Before she could drag his head back to her so they

could get started on round two, the doorbell rang. She groaned at the interruption.

"That will be the pizza," Tom said and slipped out of her.

"Way to state the obvious," she grumbled as she plastered her back to the wall in an attempt to keep herself upright. Slipping to the floor was a high option at the moment.

The doorbell rang again. "Coming," Tom called out and he pulled up his jeans.

She picked up her discarded dress and slipped it over her head. "Yes, you did."

For a split second Tom paused and looked at her, before laughing out loud. She winked and peeled herself off the wall and headed to the fridge. "Do you want another drink?"

"Sure. Grab me a beer. I'll go deal with this guy before he walks away without giving us our pizza."

Tom walked out of the kitchen and Amberley opened the refrigerator, gripping the door as if it were a life preserver and she was bobbing all by herself in the ocean.

The fact she had been able to joke with Tom after the way he'd blown her mind with out-of-this-world-sex, surprised the heck out of her. Nothing had prepared her for the way her body seemed to come alive beneath his fingers. When she'd asked to come and stay with him, she never imagined that within two hours he'd have her up against the wall pounding into her. Not that she was complaining. Her dreams about him of possessing her paled in comparison with the real thing.

A shiver wracked her body, and it had nothing to do with the cool air emanating from the fridge.

How was she going to keep her hands to herself now that she'd sampled Tom?

It seemed impossible not to jump him every single chance she got, but she had to control her urges. The whole point of this visit, apart from escaping her mother's stupid matchmaking plans, was to do research for her script. The same script that was going to catapult her into the world of screenwriting. And prove, not only to her mom, but the industry in general, that this was a serious vocation for her. She wasn't playing at it like her mom intimated.

"Ambs? Pizza's gonna be all gone if you don't come and get some. Are you having trouble finding the drinks?"

Tom voice was closer now and she looked up to see him standing in the doorway. "Um, no. No trouble." She reached in and hurriedly grabbed two bottles of beer. Normally she avoided beer, but a little alcohol may be what she needed to get herself back under control.

Mentally she laughed at herself. What an oxymoron that was, having alcohol to get herself under control. Alcohol lowered inhibitions, it didn't raise them.

A hand closed around the back of her head and the next instant she found herself wrapped up in a hug, her cheek resting against Tom's warm chest.

Sighing, she wound her arms around him, making sure to keep the cold bottles away from his bare skin. Being in his arms all her thoughts and worries drifted away and peace settled over her. If there was an option to stay in this very spot for the rest of her life, she'd tick, tick, tick it. Unfortunately, life didn't work out that way and she'd always been independent. One hot sex session with Thomas Grant wasn't going to change that.

She pressed her lips against his chest and pulled out of his embrace. "I'm starving, let's go eat."

Brushing past him she walked on shaky legs out to the living room. Resting on the wooden coffee table in the middle of the room were three pizza boxes. Sure she was hungry, but the chances of her devouring one pizza was slim, eating three —impossible.

Behind her she sensed more than heard Tom

enter the room. Glancing over her shoulder at him she quirked an eyebrow. "Expecting company?"

He laughed and the sound filled her with joy. "Nope, wanted to give you a couple of options and I'm hungry. Besides this will feed me for a couple of days."

Her good humor deflated in seconds. Did he mean he was going to take her to a hotel after all? Why else would he say that the pizza would feed him and not her. Determined not to let him see the spark of hurt his words caused she plastered on a smile. "Makes sense." She held out one of the bottles she still had a hold of. "Here's your beer."

Tom took the bottle from her, but his fingers closed over hers, effectively squashing any attempt of hers to put some distance between them. "What's wrong, Ambs?"

No way was she going to tell him about her doubts. In all the time she'd known Tom he didn't seem like the *wham bam thank you ma'am* type of guy. However, it had been years since she really spent any time with him, and she'd heard the stories about how military guys had girls in every port. Why wouldn't Tom be that way? He had the looks for sure.

"Nothing, I'm getting hangry."

"Hangry?"

"Yeah, you know, getting angry because I'm

hungry." She pulled at her hand and he relinquished the grip had on it.

His eyes narrowed as he twisted the cap off his beer bottle. A second ago his hands had had her trapped, unable to move. Now his eyes were doing the same.

Damn, what they did in the kitchen shouldn't have happened, it had wrecked the easy camaraderie they'd always had between them.

Twisting her own cap off the beer, she took a long swallow hoping it would break the spell between them. The bitter brew coated her tongue and she grimaced. "God, I hate beer."

Tom shook his head and smiled. "Then why did you grab one?"

She shrugged and, now that the sensual spell that had been woven around them had been broken, she walked to the couch. It looked like he'd ordered cheese, pepperoni, and the works pizzas. Well she planned to avoid the works, it had onion on it and the last thing she wanted was onion breath. Then again if Tom took a piece of it and then kissed her, wouldn't he have onion breath as well?

Oh my God, what the hell am I thinking. Onion breath? Am I thirteen?

Amberley picked up a piece of pepperoni and took a massive bite. At least if she had her mouth full of food nothing stupid would come out of it. She noted Tom also grabbed a piece of pepperoni, and sat beside on her on the couch their knees brushing against each other. Maybe he had the same idea as her—no onion breath.

She concentrated on eating and not the fact Tom hadn't bothered to put his shirt back on. His six pack was as distracting as a dog seeing a squirrel. How much time and effort did it take to maintain a body like that?

A hot flash of desire rushed through her at the idea of watching Tom work out. Arm muscles straining as he did push-up after push-up. His t-shirt clinging to his ripped torso the longer he did the exercises.

Could he bench press her?

Her twitter friend sent her a GIF where a guy was doing pushups over the top of a woman. Could Tom do that? Maybe naked. Maybe she could add it into her script.

Wait.

No.

Shit, having sex with him had befuddled her mind. The main reason for her visit to Tom was to get insight for her script, make it as authentic and real as possible. She didn't think the SEAL teams went around doing naked push-ups. As yet the casting hadn't been decided on. She knew the director had started to approach actors, teasing them with the synopsis and basic idea for the movie. Because Pascal was directing the movie, some actors may commit before they'd seen the script. Her job was to ensure that once they read it, they were even more committed to the project.

What she had to do was her job and not fall for Tom. She couldn't fail with this script and give her mom the satisfaction of saying *I told you so.* Which meant what happened in the kitchen earlier couldn't happen again.

No matter how temping he was.

CHAPTER FIVE

Tom went through the motions of PT on auto pilot. Not since BUD/s training had he been so exhausted, not even while on a mission. At least when he'd been away he'd been able to catch some form of shut eye, but living with Amberley, sleep had gone out the window.

Since she'd arrived, five days ago, she'd been doing everything to avoid touching him, like he carried some communicable disease. If he hadn't had scratch marks on his shoulders, he would've wondered if he'd dreamed having wild sex with Amberley in the kitchen. There'd been no more touches or kisses.

He had fully expected to ask her to join him in his bedroom after they'd eaten the pizza so he could explore every inch of her body. Instead, she'd blurted something about needing space and had all but run to the bedroom he'd shown her earlier.

"Fuck, Red, get your head out of your ass." Robot's voice thundered close by. He looked around and saw the guys all looking down at him where he'd been doing push-ups.

Quickly, he jumped to his feet. "Sorry, Robot." He withstood the gazes of his teammates, knowing that if he flinched even a little they'd be on to him, asking him questions he wasn't ready to answer. They'd already hounded him the day after Amberley arrived and his answers had been generic. At the time he knew it wasn't enough, but he still wasn't ready to be questioned about what he was doing with Amberley.

"Is there anything you need to talk about?" asked Italy.

Tom rolled his eyes. "Really? We're not a knitting club, sitting around and gossiping. We're Navy fucking SEALs. So how about we get back to doing our PT?"

He began to jog down the beach, knowing the guys would follow. Well hoping they would.

What the hell was that with Italy? Asking if he needed to talk. Over the last couple of years, with everyone finding love and getting married, it had made the guys more willing to talk about anything. Well he wasn't in that club and had no plans to join it.

If they wanted to get together and talk through their problems like they were on Dr. Phil, well all power to them. It wasn't his thing.

Thirty minutes later they all traipsed back to base to find Commander Black waiting for them.

A muttering of *shit* and *fuck* echoed around him.

"Glad to have you back, gentleman. Shower, change and meet me in the conference room for a briefing. You're going to be wheels up in four hours."

Fuck, four hours?

Tom slow jogged with the rest of his teammates toward the showers. He had to inform Amberley he was about to ship out.

How would she take the news?

Would she get on a plane and go back to LA or would she wait for him?

As if she'd wait for him, why the hell would he even think something like that? The logical thing for her would be to go back to LA. She may have been avoiding touching him, but she had talked to him about some of the things he'd gone through to become a SEAL. Asked him questions about battle scenes, the equipment they used and the atmosphere of the places he'd gone too. She'd even let him read a couple of pages, for clarification that she'd gotten terms and other stuff correct and he'd been impressed. Through her words she'd captured the essence of what it was to be a SEAL on a mission.

Now she'd be able to find out what happened when they got called up at a moment's notice. How it would affect families and loved ones knowing their men were going off to parts unknown to do things they couldn't imagine.

Which brought him back to his thoughts about how she'd react to the news. No way would she stay at his place until he returned. There was no reason and he had no idea how long he'd be gone anyway. He could be gone for a couple of days or a couple of months. It all depended on where they were going and what their mission was. Except he couldn't get the thought of walking back into his apartment and seeing her there, waiting for him, from his mind.

"What are you going to do about Amberley?" Cowboy asked as they walked toward the conference room ten minutes later.

He lifted a shoulder as if he didn't care one way or the other. "Not sure. She'll probably go back to LA. I think I've helped her enough with her script."

"Well if she wants to stay I'm sure Faith and the others will all welcome her."

No way. Not happening. He loved all the women his teammates had partnered up with, but he wasn't about give everyone ideas he and Amberley were a couple. For a few moments, that first night, he wondered if there could be something between them. After the way she fled to her room later on that night, he got the message loud and clear—there was no chance of a future for them.

"I don't think that's necessary. As I said I'm pretty sure she'll head back to LA." They'd reached the door and walked in. The rest of the team were assembled.

"Take a seat, gentleman," Commander Black said. "We've got a situation over in Africa. There's a hostage we need to get out. Time is of the essence which is why you'll be wheels up today."

"Where are we headed?" Robot asked.

"You'll be headed to Sudan. It's not going to be easy, there's a group of insurgents who have kidnapped, raped and tortured women and children. The woman you'll be rescuing is a photojournalist. The guy she was with was killed when they took her. She's been missing for two weeks."

"What the fuck, two weeks? Why wasn't action taken sooner?" T-Rex demanded, leaning forward on the table. Tom could understand why his teammate was anxious, his wife Brielle had been kidnapped and they'd been the ones who rescued her.

"I know, we've only just got the intel now." Commander Black continued, outlining the situation and where the hot zone was.

Tom listened to his commander, but half of his mind was on Amberley and how she was going to take the news. Did it even matter how she took it? They were friends and friends only. She'd come here for his help and he'd given it to her.

End of story.

Amberley stood by the door, watching as Tom moved around his room. Every step precise, and he packed with an efficiency she could only wish she possessed.

"How long will you be gone?" she asked, sure he'd told her but the second he mentioned he was leaving on a mission, white noise had filled her ears and she hadn't heard another word he said.

"I told you, I don't know. I never know how long a mission can take because there are always variables we don't know about until we get there."

Amberley wrapped her arms around her waist, wishing the tension that existed between them would disappear. It was her own fault. She'd created it by freaking out after they'd had sex. For the last week she'd lain in bed at night wishing she could walk into Tom's room and climb into his bed. Have his strong arms wrap around her.

And every night she'd talked herself out of it, saying it was better for her to keep her distance. The only good thing about the whole situation was that the words were flowing and she had a rough draft of the script almost completed. Tom had answered her questions, and given her such an insight to team dynamics that she knew it brought a richness to the script she never would've been able to achieve if she hadn't visited. Amberley hoped she'd been able to transfer that into some amazing scenes for the movie.

There was no reason for her to stay. With Tom going away it made her return to L.A. easier. But going home was the last thing she wanted to do. Her mom had been messaging her daily, wanting to know when she was returning. Amberley hadn't answered any of them.

"Amberley?" Tom's voice penetrated her consciousness dissipating her inner thoughts.

"Sorry, what did you say?"

"I asked what you were going to do?" He had a bag slung over his shoulder. Tension vibrated from him and she didn't know if it was because of his upcoming mission or because he was getting frustrated with her inattention.

"I guess I'll go back to LA. There's no reason to stay, is there?" She left the question hanging, wishing and hoping that he'd tell her she could stay until he returned. Which was completely ridiculous. Why would he want her to hang around? She'd given him no reason to believe she wanted to be with him.

"Right. Well you're welcome to stay until you get a flight out." Tom glanced at his watch and then looked at her. The message loud and clear. He needed to leave.

"Thanks, I'll—umm—I'll check out flights. I should be able to get one tonight, even if I have to deal with a couple of stops. I don't want to impose on you."

God, how she wanted him to drop his bag, frame her face with his big hands and kiss her. Ask her to stay and wait for him to return. Amberley went to take a step forward, but pulled back at the last second.

A thump was the only warning she had that something was about to happen. She gasped when Tom's hands curled around her shoulders and his lips crashed down on hers. A moan escaped from her and she aligned her body against his. Even through his uniform she could feel his muscles bunching as he tightened his hold on her.

His lips roved over hers and she opened her mouth, allowing his tongue access. God, why had she pushed him away? She could've been experiencing this for the last few days. Why had she felt the need to put distance between them when all she'd ever wanted was to be close to him? How magical would it have been to wake up in his arms? Would she ever experience it?

Fear crept over her at the thought of never being able to see him again. Knowing that when he walked out the door on his mission he may never return. Over the years the fact his job was dangerous had always been in the far recesses of her mind. But being with him and hearing him talk about the various maneuvers used in a mission the dangerous reality of his job sunk in.

Tom pulled away from her, resting his forehead against hers. "I have to go, Ambs."

"I know. Before you go I need to say something."

"What?"

Suddenly it became imperative to tell him she'd always liked him more than him just being Jenny's big brother. This could be the last time she saw him and she didn't want him to leave without knowing.

She leaned back so she was looking up at him. "I had the biggest crush on you when I was a teenager. You don't know hard it was to not jump you whenever I came over. I hated Joanna for having what I wanted."

Tom's eyes widened with her declaration. His mouth opened and closed before he spoke. "I can't believe you're telling me this as I'm about to walk out the door."

"I know, the timing sucks but I wanted you to know."

He closed the distance between them, his lips a hairs breadth away from hers. "You weren't the only one who had a crush. I wanted you big time too."

A sigh rippled through her as he kissed her once again. His touch light and gentle but full of emotion.

Why had she pushed him away? It was so stupid of her. Now he was leaving and she didn't know how long it would be before she saw him again.

Once again it was Tom who broke the kiss. "I really have to go now."

Somehow she found the strength to extract herself from his embrace, the last thing she wanted to do. Amberley reached out and placed her hand on his chest, over his heart. "When you get back, call me, okay?"

How she managed to keep a begging tone out of her voice amazed her. Standing in front of him she swallowed hard to keep the tears from falling down her cheeks.

"Yeah. You take care too. Don't let your mom set you up anymore, you're taken, remember?" He finished with a wink.

"I remember. Be careful, Tom."

Her eyelids drifted closed as he trailed a finger down her cheek. "Always."

A second later his touch was gone. She could hear the soft tread of his feet as he walked toward his door, opening her eyes in time to see him look back at her.

"Bye." She whispered.

Tom pressed two fingers to the mouth that had been ravaging her only moments ago and blew her a kiss. The door shut behind him and she grasped the imaginary kiss out of the air and held it against her heart.

She would keep his kiss safe until Tom returned and then she could give it back to him.

CHAPTER SIX

Three hours later, Amberley sat in the first class lounge at the airport waiting for her flight. She'd managed to get on a late afternoon flight out of Norfolk, landing at LAX after a stop in Denver. Not the most ideal of flights, but she'd jumped on it the moment she'd found she could get a seat.

After the door had closed behind Tom, the silence in the apartment settled around her, almost stifling her. She hadn't felt that way when he'd been at work. Maybe that was because she'd known he was on base and not off to places unknown. Doing God knows what and putting his life on the line so that she had the freedom to sit in the airport lounge, sipping champagne while she waited to go back to the fake world of Hollywood.

Her phone trilled and she placed her drink down. Glancing at the screen she saw it was director of the film she was writing the script for. She sat up a little straighter, like she was going for an interview. "Hi Pascal, how are you?"

"Good. Good. I wanted to know how you're getting on with the script. We've got a couple of people lined up and I'm hoping we can show them part or all of it."

"It's going well, I'm almost done. In fact, I'm at the airport now, heading back to LA. I land close to midnight. I can meet with you tomorrow and show you what I've got."

"You're not in LA?"

"No, I'm in Virginia. I have a friend who is military and he helped me with research about how teams work etc. I wanted to make sure what I've written is authentic and what happens during missions. I want to make this movie a success so I believed getting input from military personnel was necessary."

Silence stretched between her and Pascal and she wondered if she was about to be fired as the film's script writer. Surely he wouldn't do that to her. She was determined to make the writing amazing and she was sure she'd achieved that. Tom had helped her and the parts she'd let him read, he'd told her, her portrayal was spot on.

"Well, that's good to hear. When it comes to action movies, like the one we're working on, I want them to be as realistic as possible. I can't wait to read what you've written."

Relief poured through her and she collapsed against the back of the lounge chair she'd been sitting in. "I'm so glad. I really do think you're going to love it."

"Excellent. Why don't you come to the studio tomorrow at ten. We can look through the script. I'm trying to arrange for one of the actors to come in, so I'd like you to be present in that meeting as well."

"Definitely." The disembodied voice of the airline worker announcing her flight was ready for boarding crackled over the loud speak. "I'm sorry to cut this call short, Pascal, but my flight has been called to board."

"That's fine. I'll see you tomorrow."

"You sure will." Amberley disconnected the call and contained the urge to do a happy dance around the lounge. Pascal seemed very happy she'd taken the initiative when writing her script and she only hoped he loved it. Anything else wouldn't bear thinking about.

Taking a deep breath, Amberley raised her closed fist and rapped on the wooden door. When she'd arrived at the studio, Pascal's assistant had greeted her as she was walking out the door and told Amberley to head back to the director's office.

Tiredness pervaded her bones but she shoved it aside. She'd spent most of the night, after she landed, completing the script. Playing around with things and making sure every single word shone. The finished product, in her opinion, was incomparable to anything she'd ever written before. Her visit with Tom had inspired her, not to mention his insight had helped her create depth to the characters and the story. If Pascal loved it as much as she did, Amberley was positive her screenwriting career was about to take off.

"Come in."

Twisting the handle Amberley opened the door and walked in. Pascal was seated at a desk that was pristine. For some reason she expected it to be cluttered with scripts and other paperwork. On a shelf behind his desk stood the two Oscars he'd won for Best Director and numerous Golden Globe statutes.

One day she would have a shelf with an Oscar on it. She'd received an Emmy and Golden Globe when she'd been on the sitcom. She'd been one of the youngest stars to ever win the awards. Another reason why her mom continually pushed her to go back into acting.

Just think you could have two or more Oscars by now if you'd stayed in acting.

She heard that line from her mom so many times she was numb to it now. Acting wasn't her calling anymore, script writing was. This script she was about to hand over was going to make her career.

"Morning, Pascal, how are you?"

Pascal looked up and smiled at her. "Amberley. Great to see you. Take a seat. I'm anxious to see what you've got for me. The sample you sent when I was trying to decide who was going to work on the script was amazing. The first scene was exactly what I'm looking for. The movie needs to open big and your scene will achieve that for sure."

Pride swept through her. She'd been aware Pascal had liked what she'd written, and had known that was the reason she'd gotten the job, but hearing made her feel extremely better. "Wait until you see it now. I've made some adjustments to it after talking with my military friend. I think you'll love it even more."

Mentally she crossed her fingers that he would. There was no reason for him not to, but there was always a chance he wouldn't like it.

Pascal frowned and clasped his hands together on the shiny surface of his desk. "I didn't think it needed to be changed. I already have plans for how I'm going to shoot it."

Damn, he'd gone from being happy and excited to not so happy. "What I wrote before is still all there, I've just added a few more lines of dialogue. Things the teams say to each other. As well as expanded the scene where they're rescuing the hostages."

"Well, we'll see if the changes stay. Have you a got a copy of the script for me?"

Even though she'd already emailed a copy to his assistant and knowing she probably would've printed out a copy for Pascal, Amberley had known turning up without a paper copy for him wouldn't sit well. "Yes, I do." She reached into her laptop bag and pulled it out, along with her laptop. If Pascal had any changes she planned to make them immediately.

"Good. I've also got some casting news."

Amberley sat a little straighter. From the very beginning he'd told her people were interested but wouldn't give her names. "Fantastic. On the phone yesterday you mentioned you were hoping one of the actors would be available to meet with today. I hope they'll love the script when they read it."

Pascal chuckled. "Well this leading lady is one of the easiest actresses to work with. She'll take anything and make it gold. I'm looking forward to working with her."

"That's great, who is it?"

"Samantha Rayse."

Amberley barely contained her excitement. She'd seen some of Samantha's movies and Pascal was right. She shone on the screen. Her star was beginning to rise and this movie could send her career into the stratosphere. "That's a wonderful addition. I'll look forward to working with her."

"She's meeting us in a half hour." Pascal commented as he read through her script.

"Okay." Amberley didn't know what else to say. When she'd arrived she'd assumed she would present the script, Pascal would read over it, and that would be it. She certainly hadn't expected to meet one of the stars of the film. "Do you have any ideas on who you're looking at for the leading male character? Or who will play his teammates?"

Amberley thought back to the picture Tom had shown her of his teammates when they'd been deployed. They all looked as fit as he did. She was disappointed she hadn't been able to meet any of them when she'd been in Virginia. Of course, if he hadn't had to ship out a few days after she'd arrived, she may have met them.

For the past twenty-four hours she'd managed to

put the thought of Tom being in danger from her mind. But now that she'd thought about him, worry for him and his team was front and center.

"I'm still working on the lead actor, but I've got someone in mind. I'm meeting with his agent this afternoon." He flicked through a few more pages of the script, a pencil skimming along the typewritten lines. The fact he wasn't making any notations pleased her.

He looked at up and smiled. "I like what you've done here, Amberley. There's definitely more of a connection between the team than there was before. Who did you say your military contact was? Perhaps he could consult on set as well."

"I didn't say who he was. He's a family friend, I've known him since my high school days. And I don't think he'd be able to consult, unfortunately."

"Why not? Specialist films have always had input from experts. The fact you know someone in the military is perfect."

Amberley sighed, how much should she tell Pascal? Tom was a SEAL, their missions were dangerous and covert. She was positive they didn't like to advertise to all and sundry who they were and what they did. The fact of the matter was, she didn't know all the details about Tom's team. She knew there were various SEAL team designations.

Everyone knew SEAL Team 6 had taken out Bin Laden. Was Tom on SEAL Team 6?

"Look, Pascal, my friend is a SEAL, I don't think he'd want his identity linked to the movie. He helped me as a favor. He's also active duty and is out of the country at the moment. Even if I wanted to ask him I couldn't."

"Hmm, okay, I can understand that." A knock on his door prevented any more conversation, and Amberley was grateful for the interruption. Hopefully, whoever it was, would put him off remembering what they'd been talking about.

Amberley turned as the door opened. A tall, slender woman with dark brown hair stood in the doorway.

Samantha Rayse.

"Hi, is it okay if I come in? I'm a little early." She smiled at Pascal before turning to her. "Oh my God, you're Amberley Price. I loved watching your show. Are you going to be in this movie as well?"

Amberley laughed. "Well thank you and no I'm not going to be in the movie."

"Well darn. There goes my dream of working with one of the actors I idolized when I was acting in my high school productions." Samantha said and sat down in the chair next to her. "If you're not going to be in the movie, what are you doing here?" Her hand clapped over her mouth. "Oh shit, I didn't mean to be rude. That came out so wrong."

Amberley looked over to where Pascal still sat, amusement at the exchange between the two of them shining in his eyes. He leaned forward. "Samantha, it's good to see you and thank you for coming in at such short notice."

As if she remembered the reason for where she was, Samantha sat a little straighter and Amberley noticed a slight pink hue dusting her cheeks. "Sorry Pascal, I was just, well," she waved a hand in Amberley's direction. "I went a little fan girly."

Pascal chuckled. "I noticed, and in answer to your question as to why Amberley's here she's our screenwriter for the movie."

Samantha's eyes widened as she turned to look at her. "Really? I didn't know you wrote screenplays, Amberley."

Amberley nodded. "I've been writing for a few years now. I've done some small indie projects. But this is my first studio feature film."

"I think you're going to like it, Samantha. Amberley's written a strong female character. I know you'll bring your own unique sense of style to the character that will make her shine even more."

"Thanks, Pascal, I'm excited and nervous. I know

I'm not a big drawcard yet, but I'm going to make sure I bring your vision to life."

"With what Amberley's written, I have every faith in you being able bring the character to life." He glanced at his phone. "Now I've got to get to set for another movie. I'll leave you two to get acquainted. Samantha, if you speak to my assistant on the way out she'll give you a copy of the script. I'm excited to be working with you both."

Amberley stood when Pascal did and she noted Samantha did the same as well. They followed him out and she waited while Samantha was handed a copy of her script. Seeing her words in the hands of the actress who was playing the starring role was a surreal moment.

"Oh my God," Samantha gushed as they walked down the hallway. "I'm going to star in a movie directed by Pascal Hernandez and written by Amberley Price. Pinch me I have to be dreaming."

"Trust me, you're not dreaming because I can't believe it either," Amberley laughed. "How about we find somewhere to sit down and we can go through the script if you like?"

"Definitely. I can't wait to see what you've written."

The sunshine and warm Los Angeles air hit her the

second she walked out of the building. Looking up at the sky she wondered where Tom was and if he was okay. Was it night where he was? Was he caught up in the middle of a battle? What if he'd been hurt? How would she even know? None of his teammates knew that they had been together. Had Tom even mentioned her to them? The thoughts swarmed through her mind and sobered her excitement at meeting Samantha.

"How about we sit over there?" Samantha's words were a welcome respite from her inner turmoil. Samantha was pointing to a wooden picnic table beneath a large tree.

"Sure, sounds great." The last thing she needed to do was give Samantha the impression she was flaky. Amberley sat and laid her laptop back on the bench beside her.

"Are you okay?" Samantha asked, her fingers laced together, resting on the script.

"Sure. Why?"

"Well you kind of looked like you'd lost your best friend a few moments ago."

Amberley straightened her shoulders and pasted a smile on her face. "No. Not at all. I was thinking about a friend who's away, but I'm fine." She pulled the laptop out of her bag and lifted the lid. The machine fired up and her script appeared on the screen. "How about we go through the opening scene. Did Pascal go through the basic premise of the film?"

"He mentioned it was a military film involving a SEAL team and a rescue." Samantha commented as she turned the pages.

"And that was enough for you to say yes and sign on without reading any part of the script?"

Samantha looked up and Amberley noticed the light had disappeared from her eyes and her whole demeanor became more serious. "Yes, I didn't need anything else."

After making the decision to become a screenwriter, Amberley had become adept at reading people and situations. Donning a wig and glasses she'd gone to different malls and sat in the food court and people watched. She'd let her imagination go and came up with scenarios related to couples, families and groups of people. She'd write short plays and honed her skills while doing script writing courses.

Observing Samantha now, Amberley could tell it wasn't just the story idea that appealed to the actress, there was a personal reason for her signing on to do the movie. She didn't believe Samantha's motives were to enhance her career. It was a deeper reason. Question was, would Samantha share it with her, a person she'd just met or keep the reasons to herself and use it to fuel her performance.

If it was Amberley, she'd keep it close and draw on it whenever the need called for it. "I'm glad you took the leap of faith. Once you read the script I'm sure you won't be disappointed."

"I know I won't. After the little I've read, I know it's going to be amazing." She closed the script and looked at Amberley. "This is not something I share with everyone, but I have a feeling you and I are going to get on well. I have a personal reason for doing this movie."

Amberley mentally high fived herself for her summation of Samantha's reasoning. "I suspected."

"You did?"

"Yeah, it's the way you spoke when you told me about signing on. I'm pretty good at reading people so I figured there was a personal reason for doing it." She leaned forward and placed her hand over Samantha's. "I want to let you know that whatever you say won't be appearing on the evening gossip shows. I had a SEAL friend help me with this script. I won't ever reveal his identity to the public, unless he wants me too."

Or we become an item, but even then I'll keep Tom's job quiet unless he's happy for me to share it.

"I believe you. And thank you." Samantha reached into her bag, extracted a planner, she opened it up and pulled out a picture, sliding it across the table toward her.

Amberley picked it up. Smiling up at her were two people and looking at the smiles, she picked them as Samantha's siblings. The man in the picture was dressed in a formal military uniform, Army she thought, and the girl was dressed in what appeared to be a flight attendant uniform. "Brother and sister?" she asked, seeking confirmation of her assumption.

"Yep, they're my younger siblings. Chase, my brother, is a Lieutenant in the Army. He loves it and I'm proud of how far he's come in such a short while. He's married to an amazing woman, Sadie."

"And your sister?"

Samantha's smile softened and her finger touched the smiling woman's face. "Rayne. She's the strongest woman I know." Her voice broke as she spoke about her sister. Amberley held her breath, hoping that the next thing out of her mouth wasn't something like her sister had passed away. "She's married with a new baby. She's the reason I'm doing this movie."

"Really? Why is that?" The question popped out of her. Geez, she was sounding like a journalist, but she was really interested in the actress and her reasons for choosing to sign to the movie. The more Samantha talked, the more she could visualize her as the lead character. But still she didn't have to be rude.

"Sorry, ignore me. Your reasons for doing the movie are yours alone."

"It's fine. A couple years ago, Rayne was in Egypt and got caught up in the middle of a coup attempt. The tourist group she was with were kidnapped and imprisoned in a building."

"Oh wow, that had to be scary for them all."

"Yeah, it was. We were unaware of what happened to her until after she got back to the States. A Special Forces team, headed by her now husband, rescued her moments before she was about to be raped. Rayne has recovered and she and Ghost don't like to talk about it. Which I can totally understand. I wouldn't either."

"Ghost?" No one gave their child a name like that, did they?

Samantha chuckled. "That's the name Rayne calls him." She pointed to the script. "He's part of a team like the guys in the script. Although I think he's in the Army not the Navy like the SEALs in this movie are. He has a name like all of us, but Rayne calls him Ghost and so do I."

"Ahh that makes sense." Amberley paused, Samantha was sharing a deep part of her soul with her, she could do the same and trust her to keep it quiet. "The Navy SEAL who helped me with my script. When he talked about the other guys on his team he used nicknames too. Guess it's what they all do."

"Yeah I think it's part of what binds them close together." Samantha looked up at the sky and then back at Amberley. "Anyway, I'm doing this movie as a way of saying thank you to Ghost and his team for saving my sister. As well as honoring my brother's service to our country. Not to mention Rayne's bravery. She fought with everything in her to not let the assholes who kidnapped the tourist group, hurt her."

The love for her siblings was plain to hear in her voice. "I'm sure they're going to be thrilled you're doing this. Do you see them often?"

A shadow crossed her face, so fleeting Amberley thought she'd imagined it. "No. I—uh—couldn't make it to their weddings. I haven't met my nephew either. I've just been—" She shrugged her shoulders. "—you know busy and they live in Texas. While it's not far away, it's just better, for them, if I stay where I am. They understand, but I do miss them a lot."

Again a feeling there was more to Samantha's story filled Amberley but she let it pass. It wasn't her business. Samantha had shared a lot with her. Information she wasn't sure the actress had shared with anyone. Amberley certainly hadn't heard anything about her sister being held captive on any of the gossip sites. And if a good reporter was doing their job, they'd have dug that sort of information up. Hopefully, it would stay that way, even when Samantha made it big.

Her phone beeped and she pulled it out, hoping it was a message from Tom but didn't recognize the number. Without giving it much thought, she unlocked her phone to read the text.

I MISSED YOU WHILE YOU WERE AWAY. HOPE WE CAN CATCH UP SOON. T

A shiver of dread rolled down her spine. What the hell, Simon Wilson messaged her again? He hadn't messaged her in months, why now? She deleted the message and blocked the number.

"Everything okay?" Samantha asked.

Amberley shoved the phone back in her back. "Yeah, I'm fine." Wanting to forget all about the annoying Simon Wilson, Amberley picked up her script and smiled. "Shall we go through the first act?"

CHAPTER SEVEN

Tom slapped at the bug as it landed on his knee. "Fucking bugs. Why do they always hang the fuck around me?"

Cowboy chuckled at his side. "Because they know you're single and don't want you to feel lonely."

Tom flipped his teammate the bird and slapped another sucker away, while trying not to think about Amberley and what she was doing. Or remember what she'd told him before he walked out the door.

They'd been in Sudan for the past five days. As much as they wanted to use the intel they'd been given and extract the photo journalist, it wasn't always that easy.

As with all missions, there was a need to survey the area. Find out how many insurgents they'd have to deal with. He and his team were in pairs around the perimeter of the camp. They'd yet to set eyes on the hostage, but one particular cabin had a lot of action with men going in and out. Sometimes with a bowl, cup or both. More often than not, it was just two guys and they'd walk out, zipping up their pants laughing their heads off.

Tom was glad he wasn't teamed up with T-Rex, not that he didn't like his team mate, but this mission would have to be tough on him. Robot had paired with T-Rex, no doubt keeping his emotions in check.

A distant rumble of an engine rent the air and Cowboy straightened beside him. "Looks like there's going to be some action soon."

"Beat up jeep with two occupants and a truck bearing down fast from the east side of the camp. Be alert, and wait for my signal. Go time has arrived." Robot's low voice sounded in his ear.

With silent communication he and Cowboy took up different positions, while keeping the camp firmly in their line of business. A flurry of activity had sprung up and men began moving at a fast pace, collecting up fire arms. So far no one had entered the cabin and Tom hoped it stayed that way.

If luck was on their side the occupants of the camp would be too busy dealing with whoever was approaching, allowing Italy and Joker the opportunity to extract the hostage. Tom and the rest of his team tried not to rely on luck while on missions. Lady luck could either be a bitch or a princess. He hoped today she was feeling princess-like.

"Jeep and truck about to round the bend and arrive." This came from Joker.

Getting down on his stomach, Tom adjusted his rifle keeping his focus on the gathering men. Out of the corner of his eye he noticed Cowboy doing the same.

In that split moment before all hell threatened to break, Tom allowed himself one last thought of Amberley, hoping she wasn't having dinner with another loser her parents had set her up with. They may have only had sex one time, but it was enough for Tom to want more.

The sound of gunfire echoed throughout the camp and the people milling around the small cabins fell to the ground, some hit, some taking up positions to fire back.

"What the fuck is this? Watch your six. Don't fire back, we don't want to give our presence away. Italy and Joker, when you see your chance, get in and get out. This could be the break we've been hoping for." Amidst the chaos of gunfire Robot sounded cool and calm. The ultimate team lead and Tom was glad he'd been assigned to this team.

His finger cramped on the trigger, and he

stretched it out before crooking it again so it caressed the small piece of metal that, once depressed, could stop a man in his tracks.

The men in the truck jumped down, a couple tumbling off as they were hit with gunfire by the insurgents they'd spent the last few days watching.

"Fuck this looks like some sort of rival terrorist battle." Cowboy said. "These guys are mowing each oth—"

"Hostage secured, fall back." Italy's voice interrupted Cowboy's.

Tom crawled backward, his eyes remaining on the chaos in front of them in case one of the men took off running in their direction. When there was enough distance between the gun fight and their position, he and Cowboy stood and hot-footed it through the trees.

"Helo en route to extraction point A. ETA forty minutes." Again their team lead spoke to them.

The extraction point was the same place where they'd been dropped off. The sun was beginning to set so by the time they were picked up, the security blanket of darkness should help their escape.

The shouting and gunfire sounds faded the farther they moved away from where they'd been located. Either the battle had ended with them all killing each other, or one side won and was now dealing with the aftermath. All Tom hoped was that they wouldn't notice the hostage was now missing and come looking for them.

Thirty minutes later he and Cowboy arrived at the extraction point. A quick scan showed the positions of the rest of his team.

Over the rapid beating of his heart from running through the trees, the reassuring *thwump thwump thwump* of a helicopter reached his ears.

"Helo two minutes out. Any injuries?" Robot asked.

A chorus of negatives sounded and a little of Tom's tension receded. It wouldn't fully disappear until he was safely stateside.

The helicopter arrived and Tom crouched low as he ran to the bird, Cowboy right beside him. They climbed in and seated themselves.

The second Robot climbed on board, he thumped the roof above the pilot with his fist and the machine lifted off the ground. He then addressed Tom and the rest of the team. "Good work, we're headed to Camp Lemonnier where we'll then head back stateside."

Tom didn't need to look around to know the guys were happy to hear those words. The woman they'd freed huddled in the corner. Her clothes were tattered, hair a mass of knots and her face covered in dirt. Cowboy, the medic of the group, spoke softly to her, no doubt reassuring her that she was safe and asking if she'd allow him to look at her wounds. Her eyes darted around the space and Tom could only imagine the myriad of thoughts going through her mind. After not showering for five days he was pretty sure he and his team smelled as bad as the men who kept her captive. Not to mention how intimidating they all looked with their faces blackened out.

He saw T-Rex get up and squat in front of her as well. If anyone knew how to deal with someone so lost after an ordeal like this woman had gone through, he would. He'd brought Brielle back from the brink after she'd suffered many anxiety attacks. He could also reassure her that life won't be the same as before, but it would get better.

"Fuck, this has to be hard for T-Rex," Joker muttered beside him.

"I'm sure it's bringing back memories he'd rather do without. But having him here is probably the best for her. He can keep her attention focused on him while Cowboy checks her out."

"Yeah, there is that." Joker wiped a hand down his face. "I'm looking forward to getting back home."

A note in his tone drew Tom's attention away from Cowboy and the victim and to his team mate. "Something going on at home? Are Suzie and Emma okay?"

Joker smiled at the mention of his family. "Nah, everything's great at home. Suzie and Emma are wonderful. I just miss them is all. It gets harder and harder to leave them."

"Are you thinking of leaving the team? Does Suzie want you to do that?"

"I'd be lying if I said it hasn't crossed my mind since Emma was born. But having a child only makes me want to keep the world safe for her. Italy and I have talked about it, he feels the same and with Brielle pregnant, T-Rex is going to be having the same thoughts. Particularly after knowing what the woman we rescued went through while we were watching her."

Memories of seeing the men go in and out of the cabin flashed across his mind. How would he feel if it was Amberley in there? Her every right stolen from her. Her body being used as an entertainment tool for men who would be less than gentle with her.

His hands clenched into fists and he wanted to go back and pummel the men's faces until they were unrecognizable. He would do anything to protect Amberley.

God, he needed to see her. The second he finished his debriefing, he'd get on a plane to LA and persuade Amberley to take their fake relationship and make it a reality.

"Yeah, that's exactly why even though sometimes I want to walk away I won't. Suzie doesn't want me to either."

"Huh?" Had he missed part of the conversation with Joker while he'd been thinking about Amberley?

Joker canted his head toward Tom's clenched fists. "I see the way you're reacting. You're thinking about it being your woman in the cabin and wanting to get revenge on the motherfuckers. Trust me, it took everything in me not to storm that cabin when those guys continually walked in and out. But the outcome may not have been as successful as it was if we'd done that."

Tom nodded, they'd been on enough missions to know that a planned attack was better than a rush in guns blazing type. Still hadn't made it any easier for any of the team to sit and wait for the best time to rescue her.

Loud sobs filled the cabin as T-Rex gathered the victim in his arms. As much as Tom loved his job, it sucked balls on occasion.

Tom raised his fist and rapped on the white wooden door. Tiredness pervaded his every pore but the second he'd landed at Norfolk, his attention had been on getting back on a plane and flying to the other side of the country to see Amberley.

When he'd turned his phone back on, there'd been a couple of messages from her. The first one letting him know she'd arrived back to LA safely. The second saying that everyone loved the script and thanking him for his input.

He tried not to read too much into the second message. Part of him felt like she was saying goodbye. Like he would let that happen. Not after what he'd thought about on the helicopter. His thoughts reconfirmed his desire to make the fake relationship Amberley had told her parents about real and he wasn't wavering from that path.

Her parents, well her mother, would be more than happy for him to keep himself as far away from Amberley as possible. No way was he going to let that happen, unless Amberley answered his knock and told him to go away.

His gut clenched at the thought. What if she'd only been using him for her script? What if now that she'd gotten what she wanted, she didn't need him anymore?

"Tom? Oh my God, you're back. And you're okay." He had a split second to comprehend the door had been opened, before Amberley launched herself at him. Instinctively, his arms closed around her as

hers looped around his neck. "I'm so happy to see you."

Okay then, she wasn't going to blow him off.

"Hey Ambs," he murmured as he buried his head in the crook of her neck. He inhaled, her unique scent and relaxed as a sense of contentment washed over him. This was so right, having her in his arms. She belonged there and he was going to do everything possible to keep her there.

"I missed you," she said a second before her lips found his. Whatever had caused her to keep her distance from him after they'd had sex in his kitchen had disappeared. He couldn't be happier.

Tightening his grip on her as his mouth roved over hers, Tom lifted her feet off the ground and walked into her house, closing her door with a back kick. The second the door slammed shut he had Amberley up against the wall.

Fuck, nothing had ever felt as perfect as holding Amberley did right that second. The need to breathe was the only reason he pulled his lips away from hers.

"That's quite the welcome home," he said as he pressed a kiss to the corner of her mouth.

"You don't know how happy I am to see you."

Everything in him urged him to ask her where her bedroom was and get reacquainted with her body, explore all the places he didn't get a chance to the last time they were together, He needed to find out if what he was feeling wasn't one-sided and she felt the same way.

"Ambs, as much as I love holding you, we need to talk."

The second her arms dropped from around his neck and she stepped away, he regretted his words. He should've just acted and then they could've talked later. When they were both mellow after an amazing bout of sex.

"I know. I'm sorry that I jumped you the second I opened the door. It's just, I was worried about you. And I wasn't expecting you but it's the best surprise." She looked away as if embarrassed by her outburst.

Tom crooked a finger under her chin, waiting until her eyes connected with his. "I missed you too, Ambs. All I could think about on the way back was coming to see you. I don't know what it means, but I'm here because I want to continue what we started at my place. If I'm wrong about this and, I'll go back to the airport and get on a plane and fly home ag—" Two of her fingers pressed against his lips, halting the flow of words.

"I want that too, Tom. I'm sorry I freaked out after what we did in the kitchen that first night at your place. There were so many times I wanted to creep into your room, crawl into your bed and curl myself around you."

His body immediately hardened at her words. She was wearing the same type of flowy dress she'd worn that first night at his place. He was beginning to love them. They hinted at her curves and could be removed very quickly. "I wouldn't have turned you away if you had," he murmured answering her question.

Amberley laughed, the husky sound igniting the flames even further in him. He clenched his fists to stop himself from dragging her close again.

"I know we come from completely different backgrounds and I know I would never be your parents' choice. But I can't walk away from you. I *don't* want to walk away."

"Oh Tom, I don't want you to. I don't care what my parents think. It's my life and I want *you*."

"So are we taking fake to real?" he asked as he hooked a loose piece of her auburn hair behind her ear.

Her green eyes sparkled like the brightest emerald and her kiss-plump lips curved into a sexy smile. "We sure are. Tom will you have dinner with me?"

CHAPTER EIGHT

Amberley tossed the paper napkin into the empty pizza box. After declaring that she was on board with making her and Tom's relationship real, she pushed down the urge to drag him to her bedroom and have her wicked way with him.

There would've been no argument from Tom if she'd done that, he'd given her every indication he wanted to cement their relationship in the bedroom. But she'd wanted build the anticipation so the moment they ended up in the bedroom it would be magical. Which was why she'd invited him to dinner.

"I'm having déjà vu," he commented beside her as he copied her action of getting rid of the napkin.

"Really? Why?"

"Well that first night you arrived in Virginia we had pizza."

Amberley curled her legs up and cuddled into Tom's side. His arm immediately went around her shoulders and started to play with her hair. "From memory you ordered three pizzas, tonight we only ordered one."

"Hey, I was giving you options. Besides that fueled me and my team the next day."

She laughed. "I can't believe you guys exercise your assess off and then scarf down cold pizza."

"If you knew what we ate while on missions, you wouldn't find it strange at all."

And just like that the temperature in the room cooled a little. So far she'd been able to push aside the fact that Tom had been on a mission. "Was it really bad?" she asked. Having him beside her reassured her that he was safe, but still she needed to know.

"It wasn't as bad as some."

The news had been full of how a kidnapped photo journalist had been rescued while Tom had been away. After what Samantha had told her, her curiosity was piqued and she had to find out if Tom had been part of the rescue mission. "Where did you go?"

A shudder rippled through Tom and because she was practically in his lap, she felt every second of it. "I can't tell you. Our missions are covert for a reason.

If we're going to make a go of this, you're going to have to understand that there are some aspects of my job I can't tell you about. My missions and what we do are classified and I'll only ever talk about with my Commander and my team."

"I understand, and I'm sure I'll get used to it, but sometimes I may slip and ask."

Tom dropped a kiss on her head and she relaxed against him again. "It's okay. I know it's going to take a little getting used to."

Silence cocooned them for a few minutes. How would this relationship between them work? She lived and worked in LA and he lived and worked in Virginia. Could they do a long distance thing?

She sat up abruptly. "How long are you here for? Don't you have to be on base seeing as you just got back from a mission?"

"We usually get a couple of down days after we get back. Normally we still meet up to do PT, but I think after this trip. The guys want to spend time with their families."

In a couple of sentences, Tom had given her an insight as to how difficult missions could be on them. Without a doubt, she believed they'd been the ones who'd rescued the photo journalist. The incident reminded her of her conversation with Samantha

Rayse about her sister. And how her sister's husband was on team similar to Tom's.

"Do you work with other special ops teams from other branches of the military?" she asked.

"Sometimes, why do you ask?"

Amberley bit her lip, wishing she hadn't asked that question. She'd promised she would keep the actress's confidence and not breathe a word of it to anyone. It wasn't her story to tell anyway. "No reason, it doesn't matter."

She yelped as Tom moved her so she straddled his legs. "Tom, what are you doing?"

"If we're going to have a relationship there needs to be complete honesty between us. I know I just said I can't tell you about my missions, but with every other aspect of our lives I will be totally honest with you. Whatever you tell me will always remain between us. There has to be a reason for you to ask that question. I can see it in your eyes."

"I'm not sure I should say anything. I made a promise to someone to keep her secret."

"Ambs, it's not as if I'm a gossip reporter. Or someone who would call up an online magazine and spread rumors. I've got plenty of secrets." His hand smoothed over her head and she leaned into his palm. The touch was comforting and gave her the sense she was the most precious thing in the world.

He'd come to see her. He'd gotten off the plane in Virginia and instead of staying at his home, he'd flown across the country to see *her*. His motives for seeing her weren't because of what her parents could give him. Far from it. He wasn't using her to gain an in with a director or producer.

Tom was here because he wanted to be with her. She could trust him not to say anything. As he said, he kept plenty of information to himself.

"I know it's a lot to ask but you can trust me, Ambs, with anything. And if you don't want to say anything I'll totally respect that too."

Amberley sighed and plucked at the buttons on Tom's shirt. She could trust him. Besides the odds of him knowing this Ghost person and his team was slim. "The actress who is playing the lead role in the movie I wrote the script for, her sister was kidnapped and rescued by her now husband. She said his team pulled her sister out of Egypt before things got really nasty. Her sister was about to be raped, but the team stormed the building and rescued her and the other hostages. If it wasn't for this Ghost person, she wouldn't have her sister."

Tom's muscles went from relaxed to hard as steel in a nanosecond beneath her. What the hell? Had he been on that mission too?

She pulled away from him. "Are you okay?" she

asked, noticing even his facial features were as tight as the thigh muscles she was sitting on.

"Maybe. You said his name was Ghost?"

"Yeah, do you know him?"

"What's his wife's name?"

Knowing that in a couple of days the casting news would be announced, she was comfortable letting Tom know Samantha's name. But telling him Samantha's sister's name after she bungled and blurted out Ghost's, she wasn't sure she could, or should do it.

He sighed beneath her and his muscles relaxed a fraction. "You asked if we worked with other military special ops teams and the answer is yes. This is one mission I can give you a few details on. About a year or so ago we were on a mission where we rescued T-Rex's wife, Brielle. On the helicopter with us was a team from another arm of the military—a Delta Force team. Their team lead's name is Ghost."

Amberley gasped. "You don't think it's the same guy do you? I mean how many special forces guys across the military would have the same nickname?"

Tim chuckled. "Probably more than you think. But, if this girl's sister's name is Rayne then yep, same one. Rayne and Ghost were involved when Brielle and T-Rex got taken a few months ago."

She had to have heard him incorrectly. He couldn't have said that Brielle and T-Rex had been taken. How did a SEAL even let that happen? On top of the fact that Samantha's sister and husband were known to Tom, her mind was swirling.

Pushing away from him she disentangled herself and stood up. "This is all too much. Let me make sure if I've got this straight. You know Ghost and his team. You've met Rayne, Ghost's wife and Samantha's sister. *And* your teammate and his wife got kidnapped, I assume that's what you meant when you said they'd been taken."

"Yes to all of it."

Amberley shook her head. "This is crazy."

Tom shrugged and took a sip of his glass of water. "Not really. Sometimes special ops teams work together and then get friendly. We've worked with a SEAL team based out of San Diego a couple of times. Ghost and his team knows them well too."

"What about, you know, being all secretive and stuff."

Tom stood, closed the distance between them and slipped his arms around her waist. "Ambs, we don't talk about our separate missions. I'm sure there's stuff that Ghost and his team have done that I don't know about. Like they don't know about all the stuff we've done. At the end of the day we're all after the one goal—keep all our loved ones and their families safe. We serve our country and are damn honored to do it."

There was no mistaking the pride in his voice as his spoke. She went up on tiptoe. "Thank you for keeping me safe." She closed the small gap between them and groaned when Tom enclosed her in his strong arms.

Why had they waited so long to do this?

Why couldn't he have kissed her when they were younger? Or she could've kissed him. Jenny would've been okay with them hooking up. Maybe not straight away, but there would've been no way she would've forgotten her friendship with Jenny. Just like Tom hadn't forgotten his friendship with Darren when he and Jenny had gotten together.

The shrill of the doorbell broke through their embrace.

"You expecting anyone?" Tom asked, resting his forehead against hers.

"No. Not many people know where I live. Plus security always calls me when someone is coming to see me before letting them through. Like they did with the pizza."

"Interesting. When I said my name, they opened the gates for me and told me to *go ahead*." He cocked an eyebrow in enquiry.

Heat suffused her cheeks. "I may have put your

name on my *automatic* guest list. I have a select few that don't need to be announced.

"Well I'm glad I'm a part of the special group of people"

The doorbell rang again. Whoever it was, wasn't being very patient. Tom's muscles had tensed again and she had a fair idea what was coming next.

"I'm opening the door."

"Fine." Arguing about that would be pointless. The short time she'd spent at his house had shown her he never left his job behind. Always protecting or guarding even in the comfort of his own home. It shouldn't surprise her that he'd do it in her place, even though he'd only been there for long.

"Looks like another delivery," he said as he pulled away from looking through the peephole.

"Hmm I'm not expecting anything. The only thing I ordered was the pizza."

"Right." Tom yanked open the door with so much force, Amberley was surprised he didn't pull it off its hinges.

The delivery guy jumped back as if he was about to be attacked by a vicious dog. "I-I-I've got a delivery here for an Amberley Price." His voice broke over saying her name and she resisted the urge to roll her eyes. Thanks to streaming services a fresh batch of viewers were seeing her show. All the young actors working waitressing jobs would love to have her problem and she shouldn't react the way she did. It was just she was trying to get a new career established. She wanted to be known for more than her television show, and this movie was going to change that for her—she hoped.

"How did you get past security?" Tom demanded and Amberley watched as the guy swallowed visibly.

"Umm th-they checked my stuff and then let me through," he stammered. She decided to take pity on the guy. But she was going to speak to security about not notifying her.

She ducked under Tom's arm where he still gripped the door. "I'm Amberley Price."

The guy shoved a box and electronic signing pad at her. Tom grabbed the parcel while she took the bulky device. With a quick stroke of the pen on the LCD screen she handed it back. "Thanks."

"It's exciting to meet you, Ms. Price." He reached into his back pocket and pulled out his phone. "Can I take a selfie with you? My friends didn't believe me when I snapped them half an hour ago to say I was delivering something to your house."

Beside her she could feel the tension in Tom rising and laid a hand on his arm. Instinct yelled at her that he was about to shove the guy back on his ass and slam the door in his face. When she'd been working all those years ago, she hadn't had a reputation as a diva, and with social media these days, she had no plans on becoming a meme, GIF or the latest trending topic on twitter. "Sure." She faced Tom and gave him a slight shove in the chest. "I've got this," she muttered to him.

He gave her an intense stare before tucking the box under his arm and taking two steps back.

"Are you ready?" she asked the delivery guy, noticing the way his eyes kept darting between her and Tom. Great, there was still a chance she'd end up as a trending topic.

"Yes, Ma'am." Amberley stood next to the guy and smiled when he held his phone up. "Thank you so much, my friends still won't believe this, even with the photo. Are you going to be doing any movies or a new TV show soon? It's been a while since you've done one. Why?"

The guy peppered questions at her with all the skill of a seasoned reporter. A sense of dread swept over her. Had she been played? Had the bumbling, nervous guy he'd been when he arrived had all been an act?

"I think you're overstepping the mark. Ms. Price will not be answering those questions. Now I suggest you leave?" Tom's voice, deep and powerful, washed over her and the color leeched from the guys face.

"I-I-I'm sorry. I'll just go now." He turned and dashed down the path to where his vehicle was parked.

"Does this happen often? Why the hell didn't security notify you like they did when the pizza arrived? You do know people impersonate all types of occupations just so they can get close to their victims. Those guards should be fired."

Enough was enough.

Amberley closed her front door, whirled and poked her finger in Tom's hard chest. "Stop that right now. You don't own me. You don't get to dictate who should or should not be fired. My life is my own and I do my own thing. What happened tonight is rare. Most delivery people are much more relaxed because they do it so much. Seeing stars in their homes doesn't make them star struck like that guy."

Tom's shoulders relaxed a little and he blew out a breath, running his hand through his hair, giving it a just out of bed look. Now that was a look she'd like to give him herself. "I'm sorry. You're right. It's just I didn't like how he invaded your privacy like that."

"Comes with the territory." She held out hand for the box he was still holding. "Can I have my parcel now?"

"Sure." He held up to his ear before turning it over in his hands. This time she rolled her eyes.

"Aren't you being a little extra?"

"No. Besides you said you weren't expecting anything. And it's after eight, not exactly delivery hours."

She reached out and took the box from Tom before he could open it himself. "Check all the delivery company websites, you'll see most will say they'll deliver up to nine in the evening." Amberley walked into the kitchen to get a knife so she could slit the tape. When she turned she almost stabbed Tom, he was that close to her. "I'm perfectly capable of opening a box. I don't need any help."

"Right, sorry." He shook his arms out and when he cocked his head to the left she heard it crack. "Sometimes it's hard to switch off after a mission. I'm hyperaware of everything for a couple of days upon my return."

Placing the knife and box on the bench she closed the distance between them. If she wanted a relationship with Tom, and she certainly did, helping him after he returned home from missions would become a priority. She would do whatever was necessary to help him adjust. The parcel could wait, Tom couldn't. She smoothed her hands up his arms, looping them around his neck.

"Maybe I can take your mind off things for a little while." Without giving him a chance to respond she pressed her lips against his. His mouth opened immediately beneath hers at the same time his own arms closed around her, holding her tight against him.

She would talk to him about what happened with the delivery guy, but not now. In the grand scheme of things it wasn't something that had to be sorted out that very minute. All that mattered to her was Tom. Amberly broke the kiss and looked up at him. "Take me to bed, Red."

His eyes widened at her request and the use of his nickname. "Anything for you, babe."

She yelped in surprise when he scooped her up in his arms.

"Where's your bedroom?" he asked as he strode out of the kitchen and back into the hallway.

"Upstairs and last door on the left." Her heart leaped out of her chest. Finally, Tom was going to be hers.

CHAPTER NINE

The second Tom stepped into Amberley's room, a sense of peace washed over him. It wasn't the tasteful pale green comforter on the bed. Or the beautiful wooden furniture that was scattered about the room. It was the woman in his arms.

His Amberley.

His body hardened even more at his possessive thought. Yes, she was his and he had no plans to let her go.

Tom set her on her feet and then pulled the comforter back, the decorative pillows bouncing down the bed.

"Your technique needs a little work there, soldier."

"Babe, I'm not a soldier, I'm a seaman. Don't get the two mixed up."

She blinked a couple of times at him. "There's so much I could say here, but I won't."

He laughed loudly. Already the tension from the mission and the way the delivery guy acted around her, melted away. "Like I haven't heard them all before." He hooked an arm around her waist and pulled her against him. "Let me show you just how good of a seaman I am."

A shiver rippled through her and his dick pushed against the zipper of his jeans. "I can't wait."

Tom released his grip on her and bent to pull his shoes and socks off. His hand went to his waist band and he flicked open his jeans, relieving a bit of the pressure off his cock. He pulled his shirt up over his head, and a low moan of appreciation came from the bed. He couldn't wait to feel her hands all over him. Their time in his kitchen hadn't been long enough. Now, here in her bed, they both would have time to explore each other.

Once he had his shirt off he looked up and saw that Amberley had removed her dress, leaving her only in a scrap of black lace. Her nipples peaked, as if she'd been caressing them while he'd been busy taking off his shirt.

"God, you're beautiful," he whispered as he

removed his jeans and climbed on the bed. His dick strained against the cotton fabric of his boxer briefs.

"I need you, Tom. I've spent the last week and half dreaming about you. Now I want the reality."

Amberley was right, he had wanted to take his time with her, but her words set him on edge. He knew if he entered her, he'd probably lose his load straight away.

He crawled up until he was over her, his arms on either side of her shoulders. "I'm real, babe." He closed the gap and pressed his lips against her. A full body shudder ripped through him. Nothing had ever felt as right as kissing Amberley did right now.

Her fingernails dug into his biceps and he didn't care if she left marks on his arms. He was more than happy to be branded by her.

He was hers.

He swept a hand down the side of her body, until he connected with the waistband of her panties. Hooking a finger beneath it, he tugged and she lifted her ass, allowing him to push the fabric down her legs. Kissing his way up her inner thigh, careful not to touch her pussy, no matter how much he wanted too. He trailed kisses over her belly until he found one breast. He sucked the pebbled peak into his mouth and Amberley moaned out loud, arching her back beneath him. His free hand massaged her other breast, plucking at her nipple while he continued to suck the other.

After a while he switched sides. By now Amberley clutched at his shoulders, lifting her hips and rubbing her pussy against his thigh.

God, he wanted to make her come. Wanted to make her scream his name as his fingers stroked in and out of her.

Keeping his mouth firmly focused on one breast his hand slipped down her body until he found the juncture between her thighs. He slipped one finger between her slick folds, her inner muscles clenched around him.

“Babe, you’re so wet.”

“All for you, Red. Only for you.”

Fuck, he couldn’t wait any longer. He needed to possess her. He stroked his fingers in and out of her a couple more times before pulling and hopping off the bed.

“Where are you going?” Amberley moaned.

“Condom.” He grabbed his jeans and pulled out his wallet, grabbing the square packet. In one motion he thrust his boxers down and ripped it open. He rolled it on as he got back on the bed. When he settled himself between her thighs he framed her face so that she was looking at him.

“I need you, Ambs.”

Her fingers brushed against his cheek and she smiled up at. "I'm all yours."

Reaching down he guided the tip of his cock to her entrance and with one fluid movement entered her. They both groaned once he settled himself fully in her.

This was how it should be between them. A soft mattress under them instead of a hard wall. Tom started to move slowly in and out of her. Her hips chasing him, wanting to keep him connected to her.

His mouth found hers as he continued their slow, sensual ride to completion. Her breathing quickened and he could tell she was close to her climax.

"Oh yes, Tom. Harder. Harder."

He raised himself up on his elbows and increased his pace. His own orgasm was so close, but he didn't want to come without her. He reached down in between them, finding her clit and circling it with his thumb. It was enough to set her off, her muscles clenched on his cock and it set off his own release. He shouted her name as he thrust one more time, holding himself still over her as he pulsed into the condom.

His arms shook with the effort to keep from falling on her. "That was amazing, Ambs."

Her lips peppered kisses over his neck. "Yes, it was perfect."

Sighing he wrapped his arms around her and rolled them so they were laying on their sides, facing each other.

Tenderly he brushed a strand of her hair off her face. Amberley was weaving her way into his heart. No, that was bullshit, she'd always been there, he was just allowing his feelings for her to come to the surface.

He wanted her in his life and he would do whatever he had to, to keep her there.

A low moan woke Amberley. It took her a few seconds to work out why she felt so hot. Tom had her wrapped up in his arms, arms that were tightening with each passing second.

"Tom," she called gently, not wanting to shock him awake should he lash out and hurt himself. Or her.

During their talks, Tom had mentioned how they all suffered from various forms of PTSD. After everything they saw and the things they had to do on their missions it was likely they all had demons to fight. She would've been more surprised if he told her he didn't suffer from PTSD.

Tom moaned loudly beside her. She reached out

and touched his forehead. Moisture beaded across his hot flesh.

Working her way out of his embrace, she sat back on her haunches and ran a hand down his chest. Maybe soft, soothing movements would wake him and make whatever demons he was fighting disappear.

"Tom, wake up. You're here, with me. Amberley. You're safe."

A second later his eyes flicked open. "Ambs?"

"Yeah, hon, I'm here. You were dreaming I think."

He scrubbed a hand down his face. She maintained her touch on his stomach. Her fingers gliding over the ridges of his six pack.

"Sorry you had to see that. As I said, it takes a few days to unwind after coming back from being away."

"You don't ever have to apologize to me, Tom. I get it. I really do. I'd be worried if you didn't have a few demons to fight." She finished by voicing her earlier inner thought.

He reached up and wound some of her hair around his fingers. "Come here."

She lay down, resting her head on his shoulder, and throwing an arm across his chest. "You don't ever have to hide who you truly are in front of me, Tom."

"Thank you," he murmured.

"Go back to sleep now, I'll keep you safe."

Amberley tightened her arms around, giving him something he'd never willingly ask for.

She lay there watching him sleep knowing with every rise of his chest she was falling more and more in love with Tom.

Amberley closed her eyes, happy she'd taken the plunge and lied about having a relationship with him. It was the best lie she'd ever told.

"Are you going to open the package you got last night?" Tom asked as he sat at the small table she in the small nook in her kitchen.

Amberley glanced over to the cardboard box sitting where she'd left it the previous evening. "I probably should. If I remember I was about to open it and then I got side-tracked."

Tom smiled, the corner of his eyes crinkling. "I'm more than happy to keep you side-tracked."

Amberley threw a piece of toast at him before getting up and grabbing the box. It wasn't huge and it was light. She had no idea what it was and who sent it to her. An uneasy feeling settled in her stomach. Simon had been texting her again, even though she constantly told him to leave her alone and blocked his number, threatened him, again, with a restraining order, he hadn't given up. What did the guy have? A collection of burner phones he continually used? That was the only explanation she could come up with as to how could he have so many numbers.

"Everything all right, Ambs?" Tom's hands landed on her shoulders.

"Yeah, I was just trying to remember if I did order something. Maybe Mom ordered it as a surprise." As if her mother would do something like that. Bettina wasn't known for her spontaneous gifts for her daughter.

"I'm pretty sure you don't believe that." Did the guy have mind reading abilities? The box was taken out of her hand before she could say anything more. "Let me open it."

She couldn't deny relief flowed through her when Tom grabbed the knife she'd taken out the previous evening to open it.

It was so stupid to be feeling this way. If Tom wasn't here she'd be opening the box herself. Would've opened it the previous evening.

"Stop." She all but shouted at him. Tom's hand hovered above the brown tape, the tip of the knife about to breach it.

"What? What's wrong?"

"This." She waved her hand at him. "If you

weren't here I'd be opening the box myself. So hand it over and let me do it."

"But I am here, so I can do it for you," he argued.

Of course he'd go all alpha male/Navy SEAL on her. But she was no shrinking violet. She'd survived numerous years of the paparazzi and fans hounding her and wanting to get her attention. She could damn well open her own box. "Tom, seriously, hand it over."

He stared her down, using a look she was sure he gave to the bad guys to get them to spill all their secrets to him. Only she wasn't a bad guy and there was no way she was going to let him intimidate her. Placing her hands on her hips, she straightened her spine, and glared right back at him.

The corners of his mouth lifted slightly. "I think I've met my match."

Amberley scoffed at that. "Yeah right. I don't think you'd cave that quickly if you were going after a terrible person. But in this situation, yes you have met your match."

Tom slid the box over the quartz counter top and handed her the knife. "Thank you," she said, a hint of smugness entering her voice.

She slit the tape and opened the flaps. Like with anything, half the box was filled with packing peanuts.

"What is it?" Tom asked.

"Don't know, there's so much packing stuff in here it's hard to see anything." Amberley reached and closed over something small and hard. Pulling it out, she held up a figurine of a girl holding a notepad and pen. It was silver and was about four inches tall. "Oh wow this is beautiful."

"It is. And appropriate too, it looks like she's writing a story."

"Yes," she whispered and traced her finger along the lines of the girl, then traced the pen and little note book a couple of times. Her finger snagged on some rough metal and tore a bit of her skin. "Ouch. I won't be touching that area again."

Amberley looked at her finger and noticed she'd cut herself and it was beginning to bleed. Before she could think Tom grabbed her hand.

"Let me look after this." Not giving her a chance to argue with him, he took the figurine out of her hand and placed it on the counter, before marching her over to the sink where he proceed to wash away the blood.

"I could've done this myself, you know. It's not like it's a major cut or anything. It's just a scratch."

"I know. But I'm here and I want to take care of you."

And there it was, the Navy SEAL again. She shook her head at him. If she was going to get involved with Tom, then she would have to get used to him taking care of her. "You're going to do this whenever I get hurt, aren't you?"

"Yup." He wrapped a piece of paper towel around her finger. "Now where's your first aid kit? I think you should put some antibiotic cream on it."

"For goodness sake, aren't you ov—" A wave of dizziness washed over her and she swayed a little. "Whoa, that's different."

"Ambs? Are you okay?"

Amberley lifted her gaze to Tom and squinted, why where there two Tom's? Another wave of dizziness hit her and she tried to reach for him, but it was like her arms weren't getting the message from her brain.

Her vision became clouded with black spots. "I don't fe..." Her knees buckled and the last thing she heard was Tom calling her name again before she sunk into a dark abyss.

CHAPTER TEN

Tom's heart leaped into his throat as he caught Amberley before she fell to the ground. "What the hell?"

He carefully laid her down on the tiled floor, before placing two fingers on her carotid artery. He released a breath when her felt her steady pulse.

"Amberley, wake up, babe." He brushed his fingers down her cheek. She remained unresponsive. "Fuck."

The last thing he wanted to do was leave her but he needed to call 9-1-1. Something wasn't right here. Why the hell had she passed out like she had? It couldn't be from lack of food because he'd seen her eat the eggs, bacon and toast they'd prepared together.

Touching the side of her neck again, reassuring

himself that her heart still beat strongly he stood and strode into the living room where he'd left his phone. Picking it up he punched in the numbers. He gave his name to the operator and quickly explained the situation while he unlocked the front door. The woman on the other end of the phone advised she'd send out an ambulance as quickly as possible.

He raced back to the kitchen, hoping that while he'd been on the phone Amberley had woken up. Unfortunately she was still out cold on the floor. Had she got paler since he'd been gone? It didn't seem possible but the closer he looked he could definitely see that she had lost more color in her face.

This time he picked up her hand to check her pulse. Instead of being strong and steady like the previous times he'd check, it was erratic.

"Fuck, what the hell happened. Ambs?" Concern rushed through him and he wished Cowboy was there. As the team's medic, he could be working on Amberley to help her.

A phone shrilled through the house and it took Tom precious seconds to work out it was probably the guard house calling Amberley. He looked around the kitchen and spied a phone on the wall. He rushed over to it and picked it up. "Hello?"

"This is Chuck from the guard house, did one of you call an ambulance?"

"Yes, I did, Amberley's passed out. Let them in."

"Certainly, sir. I'll notify Mr. and Mrs. Price as well." The guard hung up before Tom could thank him. He'd been so concerned about Amberley he hadn't given any thought to contacting her parents.

If they didn't want her seeing him before, there was no way they'd be happy with their relationship now. Their only child had gotten hurt on his watch and he had no fucking idea what the hell had happened. One minute she was fine, admiring the gift she'd been given, the next she was collapsing at his feet.

Something niggled in the back of his mind, but he couldn't grasp it as the wail of approaching sirens diverted his attention. Placing a kiss on her forehead he noticed her skin was clammy. It was like she was getting worse with every passing second.

Getting to his feet he rushed to the front door, yanking it open so quickly the paramedic that was about to knock on the wood almost fell forward.

"Are you Tom Grant? Did you call 9-1-1?"

"Yes I am and I did. You need to come quick, she's in the kitchen and getting worse by the second."

Tom stepped to the side and allowed the two paramedics to enter the house. While everything in him screamed to follow them he could see two people racing toward him.

Amberley's parents.

"Where is she? What did you do to her?" Bettina demanded the second she reached the front door.

"She's in the kitchen, help is in there with her. And I didn't do anything. I would *never* hurt, Amberley." He clenched his fists to stop himself from punching the door. How dare Bettina think he'd do anything to hurt Amberley. Hell he loved her.

Shit.

He loved her.

He'd been half in love with her when he'd been in high school. His crush hadn't died when he started dating Joanna or even when he joined the Navy. His feelings had only been buried deep and the second Amberley reached out to him the first time all those months ago, they returned with the maturity of adulthood.

While he'd been on his most recent mission, those times in the dead of night when everything was quiet, thoughts of Amberley had entered his mind. The way she smiled. The way she laughed when he made a lame joke. The feel of her body against his as he drove into her and made her his. Because she was his.

A hand touched his arm, jolting him back to the here and now. He looked up and found Amberley's dad standing in front of him.

"I'm sorry for what Bettina said. I know you won't do anything to hurt my daughter. It's written all over your face how important she is to you."

"She is. Really important."

"Bettina will see that you're the right person for Amberley."

Tom bit back a scoff. Now was not the time to remind him that his wife thought Tom was exactly what Amberley didn't need. All that mattered was Amberley and getting her well again.

The sun shone in the ER's waiting room, brightening up the place, but the occupants paid it no mind. Tom paced around the space glancing at the door every few seconds. Bettina and John sat on the plastic chairs, holding each other's hands. Looking at the couple he could see that they weren't together merely for publicity's sake. They genuinely loved each other. John was murmuring in Bettina's ear and she was leaning on him, taking the support he silently gave.

"How much longer," he muttered to no one in particular.

"It hasn't been that long, I'm sure they're doing everything they can. Are you sure you can't think of anything she may have eaten or drunk that could've caused her to pass out?"

Tom shook his head. He'd been trained to be level-headed in high stress situations. To observe and take in everything around him. But this was Amberley, nothing made sense to him. "We ate and drank the exact same thing and there's nothing wrong with me. I don't understand any of this. She was fine one minute, the next she was swaying and then collapsing at my feet."

The feeling he was missing what should've been obvious niggled at the back of his mind. He closed his eyes, and concentrated on his breathing in an attempt to clear the clutter in his brain. In his mind's eye he replayed the scene over and over. The way she smiled with delight when she opened the box and saw the silver figurine. How she traced the contours of it, admiring how sweet it was. Then pulling her finger away after cutting it. Him washing the small wound.

The answer was a shadow in his mind, right there, but just out of reach.

"Mr. and Mrs. Price?"

Tom's eyes flicked open the second the doctor spoke. He noted Amberley's parents were now standing but hadn't made a move toward the doctor, as if fear rooted them to the spot.

"Yes. What can you tell us about our daughter?" Bettina finally spoke, except where her voice usually held the tone that she wasn't to be argued with. This time she spoke quietly.

The doctor walked forward holding out his hand which both Bettina and John shook. "I'm Dr. Branston, I'm the attending ER registrar on duty when they brought your daughter in. At the moment we don't know exactly what's going on. We're running tests and Ms. Price is still unconscious."

Bettina's legs buckled and Tom was by her side in a flash propping her up. John appeared to be in shock and hadn't noticed that his wife was struggling with the news of her daughter not being awake. She gripped his arm like he was an anchor in the midst of choppy seas. Tom placed his free hand over hers and squeezed it. As hard as it was for him to know that Amberley was sick, it had to be even harder for her parents. She was their only child. And while she may grumble about how they treated her and some of the things they were doing, he knew Amberley loved them the way they loved her.

"Is there anything else you can think of that may be of use to us?"

Tom cleared his throat and the doctor made eye contact with him. "I was with Amberley when she was collapsed. She'd cut her finger on a small figurine she'd been given. I washed the wound and was asking if she had a first aid kit when she passed out." This was the same information he'd given the 9-1-1 dispatcher, but he wasn't sure if it had been relayed to the paramedic team and if they'd passed the information onto the doctor when they arrived with Amberley.

"Right, I noticed the cut as I was examining her but didn't think anything of it. I'll check again to see if there is a piece of metal buried in the skin. However, that's not likely to cause her to react the way she has. We're running tests and screening for toxins of any sort."

"Do you think she's been poisoned somehow?" he asked. Doing what he did for a living he'd seen and heard plenty. They'd closed down many chemical weapon factories where poisons were being developed that could kill on contact with the skin. It was scary to think about what could happen when someone touched something without them being aware of the danger.

Touch something without anyone being aware of the danger.

Fuck. The figurine. It couldn't be that could it?

"I think I know what's happened." He extracted

himself from Bettina's grip. "I'll be back and I'll be bringing something for you to test."

"Um, okay." The doctor's words reached him as he exited the room. His large steps eating up the distance from the waiting room to the hospital's exit.

The second he stepped outside he paused and looked up at the blue sky. "Hang on, Ambs. Please, hang on," he whispered.

Forty minutes later Tom strode back into the hospital, the figurine in a plastic zip lock bag. He headed for the waiting room, hoping that Bettina and John would still be there. He stopped abruptly when he found it was full of people, but not the couple he wanted.

Damn, why hadn't he just stopped at the triage desk and asked for the doctor instead of going off half-cocked into the waiting room thinking that was the most logical thing to do. He also had no idea which cubicle Amberley was in. She'd been whisked away on arrival and he and her parents were shown to the waiting room. Her dad had broken land speed records to keep up with ambulance so that they arrived at the hospital at the same time.

Backtracking he stopped at the desk. "I'm looking for Amberley Price, can you tell me where she is please?"

The nurse looked up at him. "Are you a relative?" she asked.

If he said no, he wouldn't be allowed up, he could lie and say he was her husband but he didn't want to do that either.

"Not technically. I'm her boyfriend and I was here with her parents earlier, but I had to go back to the house to get something. I need to see her or her parents or Dr. Branston. It's really important. It could help them work out what's wrong with her."

"I can vouch for him." Tom turned to see a paramedic who'd attended Amberley. "he rode the ambulance with us."

The nurse raised her eyebrow and looked between him and the paramedic. "Fine. She's been transferred up to ICU on the sixth floor."

Tom could've leaned over the counter and kissed her, but he controlled himself. "Thank you. I appreciate it." He turned to man standing at his side and gave him a chin lift in thanks.

Seconds later he was in an elevator heading up to the ICU. Every second it took him to get close to her could be a second off her life. The doors whooshed open and the atmosphere in the area pressed down on him. It was incredibly quiet, like everyone was afraid to speak. It made sense though because the people on this floor were fighting for their lives. The woman he loved was among them. He gripped the plastic bag a little tighter.

Tom couldn't understand why he hadn't collapsed as well. He'd touched the figurine, too, although his contact had only been brief and at the base of the object. Had Amberley absorbed whatever had been put on the small trinket? Is that why it hadn't affected him? Or when she cut her finger, had that increased her absorption rate of whatever substance had covered it? He was making an assumption that some sort of toxin had been smeared over the metal figure. It was the only thing that made sense to him.

God there were so many scenarios and he could spend time analyzing the whys and wherefores later. The most important thing he had to do was to find the doctor and tell him his suspicions.

He turned the corner and to his right was another reception area, not as large as the one in the emergency room, and only manned by one person instead of three. Taking a deep breath he approached. The woman looked up and smiled at him.

"Can I help you?"

Tom placed the zip lock bag on the counter top. "I need to see Dr. Branston. It's important, and has to do with his patient Amberley Price."

"Dr. Branston is an ER physician. You would need to go to the ER to speak to him. Once a person is transferred to the ICU another doctor is appointed as the primary physician."

"Right, well then I need to see that doctor. It's extremely important. I may have information on what is causing Ms. Price to be ill." Tom surprised himself at how calm and in control he sounded. His heart was racing and what he really wanted to do was march down the hallways, looking in every room until he found Amberley. Being away from her was killing him. He needed to touch her, to see her chest rising and falling. See her beautiful green eyes sparkle with laughter and desire. He wasn't sure what he'd do if anything happened to her.

"I'm sorry, sir, unless you're immediate family I can't give you any information. You are welcome to wait in the ICU waiting room." She pointed to the hallway on her left.

Well aware that she was only doing her job, Tom couldn't help but get frustrated with her blocking him. As much as he hadn't wanted to go down this route downstairs, right now he would if it meant saving Amberley. Saying a quick, mental apology for the lie he was about to tell he took a deep breath before speaking. "Look I couldn't have got up here if someone downstairs didn't vouch for me. I think the reason she's sick is because of this." He pointed to the bag. "Please tell me where she is and where I can find her doctor."

The nurse eyed him suspiciously, her gaze flicked between him and the bag. "Fine. She's in cubicle six, down that corridor." She pointed to her right this time.

Tom could've leaned over and kissed her, too, but didn't want to press his luck. "Thank you."

Scooping up the bag, he marched down the corridor to the right of the desk. Amberley was in the third room on the left. All around him he heard the rhythmic beep of heart monitors, a reassuring sound to everyone visiting loved ones. As he reached Amberley's room, he paused, composing himself, preparing for the sight of Amberley lying on a bed, tubes coming out of her. It was a vision he didn't want to see.

Pulling open the curtain he noticed that John and Bettina were seated by the bed. A nurse fiddled with the IV at the top of the bed, by Amberley's head. His beautiful girl's eyes were shut and her skin color was still as pale as it had been downstairs. He had hoped that whatever fluids they pumped through her would've given her cheeks a slight pink hue.

"Thomas, what do you have in your hand?"

Tom redirected his attention off Amberley and to her mother. He lifted the bag. "This is the figurine that was delivered to Amberley last night. After she opened it this morning, she ran her fingers all over it, tracing it's shape. When she got to the notepad the figure is holding she cut her finger. Not long after that she collapsed. I think whoever sent this covered it in some sort of toxin or poison."

Bettina gasped and grabbed her husband's hand. "You can't be serious. Who would do such a thing?"

Suddenly the steady beeping from the heart monitor changed pace and became more erratic. Tom's heart leaped to this throat. A silent cry of *No* echoed around his mind.

"I need you all to leave now." The nurse demanded as she depressed a button on the console above Amberley's head. She looked at Tom. "Leave that bag on the end of the bed. I heard what you said and will let the doctor know."

Tom did what the nurse said and placed the bag by Amberley's blanket covered feet. "Come on Mr. and Mrs. Price we need to let the staff do what they're trained for."

He said the words as gently as possible, when he wanted to rail at the staff for not being able to fix the woman he loved. Bettina looked like she was going to dig her heels in and not leave, but John whispered in her ear and she nodded. It killed Tom to walk out of the room, but knowing that the doctor would be walking in soon and the nurse would relay the information he'd provided, comforted him a little.

"Let's go to the waiting room." He suggested and headed in that direction, hoping Amberley's parents followed.

Like the room downstairs, the area was furnished with rows of plastic chairs lining the walls. Unlike downstairs, a couple of couches were situated in the middle of the room. In one corner was a fridge which contained bottled water and sodas. There was also a sideboard which had a coffee machine and a plastic case containing various pastries. Food was the last thing on his mind. Anything he ate would probably come straight back up or sit in his stomach like a rock.

"Can I get you anything to eat or drink?" he asked the couple once they'd seated themselves on one of the couches.

"No, thank you." They both said in unison. Another indicator of how in tune the couple were. If only the gossip magazines who'd declared the Price's marriage wasn't a love match anymore could see them now. Both were leaning on each other for support. Their relationship was the type his parents had, and the type he wanted. And what he wanted with Amberley.

His back pocket vibrated and he pulled out his phone, seeing Robot's name flash on the screen.

Fuck, he hoped they weren't about to be called back on a mission. If they were he wouldn't go. For the first time in his career, he didn't want to be called away. The team would have to make other arrangements. Maybe they could call in one of the guys who'd taken Joker's place when he'd been recovering from his gunshot wound. No way was he going to leave Amberley's side. Not while she was so sick. He'd take whatever punishment was dished out to him.

Thoughts of declining the call flitted across his mind, but he banished them quickly. Sure, he may not want to leave, but he wasn't going ignore his team lead.

Connecting the call he strode to the corner of the room. "Now's not a good time, Robot."

"What's going on, Red?"

Tom scrubbed a hand down his face. "Are you calling to tell me we have to go on a mission or are you calling to chat? Because if it's the former, I'm not going with the team. If it's the latter, as I said, it's not a good time."

"We're not going on a mission. I'm standing at your front door, and you're not here. So where are you and what's going on?"

Tom sighed, relieved that he wouldn't have to face

the Commander and explain why he refused to go on a mission. "I'm in LA, and I'm in a hospital."

"Fuck, man, what the hell happened?" Robot yelled and Tom held the phone away from his ear. "Are you all right? I can be on the next flight out if you need me to be."

"I'm fine. Amberley's in the hospital. Shit, Robot, she fucking collapsed in my arms. One minute she was talking to me, the next I was catching her as she crashed to the floor."

"I didn't realize you were visiting Amberley." His team lead's words were innocuous but there was a ton of speculation in them as well. No time like the present to let Robot know the last man standing on the team had fallen. He had no issues falling either, he only hoped Amberley was feeling the same way. He'd ask her when, not *if* she woke up, but definitely when.

"Yeah, I needed to see her. I caught the first flight out following our debriefing of the last mission."

"You know if you need us we'll be there." Robot said, clearly understanding the situation and what his words meant.

While he and Jenny had a close relationship as siblings, it wasn't like the relationship he had with his teammates. He'd dropped everything when Cowboy had needed him not that long ago, in fact the whole team had. And as much as he wanted the guys with him, they deserved to be with their families.

"Nah, I know everyone needs to be where they are right now. But thanks." Movement out of the corner of his eye caught his attention. A doctor was standing in the doorway and the way John and Bettina jumped off the couch, this must be the attending physician on Amberley's case. "Look the doc's here. I gotta go. Thanks for the call."

He disconnected the call before Robot could say anything else. In a few strides he was standing beside Amberley's parents. He held out his hand to the man. "Hi, I'm Tom Grant, I was with Amberley when she collapsed. I also brought the figurine in, were you able to find out anything?"

"Dr. Wortham," he grasped Tom's hand briefly then released it. "At the moment, Amberley has stabilized, but is still unconscious. I've sent the statue to toxicology for them to run some tests on it. I've requested the tests be a top priority so that we can get the results and start treating her."

"How long before you know anything, doctor?" John asked.

"I'm hoping we hear something within the hour. We've taken a sample of Amberley's skin from the area around the cut on her finger. I'm aware you washed the wound, but I'm hopeful, with the severity of her reaction, that we can get some insight as well."

"Can we go back into the room?" Bettina asked. Gone was the A-list Hollywood actress. A mother stood in front of the doctor, begging to see her daughter. Any animosity he felt toward the other woman and her matchmaking schemes disappeared in a second. How could he dislike a woman who clearly loved her daughter this much?

He couldn't and when Amberley was on the road to recovery he'd tell her all about how much of a mother her mom had been in the crisis.

"I think it's best if we keep the visitors to a minimum. One at a time and only for short intervals until we know exactly what we're dealing with."

Tom wanted to be the one to go into her room and sit by her bedside. Only he knew that, as much as he was softening toward Bettina, he didn't think she was totally on board with him being with her daughter regardless of the fact that he'd gotten her to the hospital as quickly as possible and had maybe found what was causing Amberley's illness.

"I'll wait here," he said. "I know the doctor only said one at a time, but I don't think he'll have too much of an issue if you both go in at the same time."

He took a step back from the couple, when he wanted to do the exact opposite.

"Thank you, Thomas." Bettina's mom came over to him. When her arms enclosed him in a hug he reflexively returned the embrace. "I underestimated you and your feelings for my daughter. We won't be long and then you can sit with her."

A few minutes later he had the room to himself and his thoughts. He closed his eyes and raised his head toward the ceiling. "Please let her be all right," he whispered.

CHAPTER ELEVEN

Awareness seeped into Amberley. Her body ached and opening her eyelids seemed impossible. A constant *beep beep beep* sounded around the room, and seemed in time with the beating of her heart.

Her mouth was dry, as if she'd been walking in Death Valley without any water for hours. She swiped her tongue over her cracked lips but that didn't seem to make any difference. The only way to find out what was going on was to open her eyes, no matter how difficult it proved to be.

The first thing that greeted her was a ceiling that didn't look like the one in her bedroom. Was she in a hotel? Had she gone on a bender the night before and gotten so drunk she passed out?

Being in a hotel wouldn't explain the constant beeping. Swiveling her head to the left she spied a bank of machines.

Hospital.

She was in hospital.

Amberley closed her eyes again, willing her mind to remember what she'd done that could've led her to ending up in a hospital bed. Her mind drew a blank and the longer she tried to think the more it began to throb.

The possibility that she'd gotten drunk and needed hospital care seemed unlikely. She'd never let herself get that wasted.

Opening her eyes again she looked to her right and spied someone slumped in a chair. His legs were crossed out in front of him and one arm hung to the side, as if it had been resting on the bed but when he'd fallen asleep it had slipped off.

Her vision was improving the longer she kept her eyes open and his facial features became recognizable to her.

"Tom?" With her throat so dry it was like she'd just mouthed his name instead of speaking it.

She tried again. "Tom." Barely a whisper but his eyes popped open and connected with hers.

"Ambs?" He got up and leaned over her, touching

something above her head. She heard a faint buzz. "You're awake?"

Close up she could see the scruff on his face, as if he hadn't shaved in a few days. "What happened?"

"How much to do remember?" he asked and she didn't like that he was avoiding answering in her question.

"I don't remember much which is why I asked you what happened." The more she talked the stronger her voice became, but her throat was still really dry. "Can I have some water please?"

"Shit, sorry. Yeah, hang on." He walked over to the sliding table and grabbed the jug, pouring water into the glass. His movements were smooth and she admired the way his t-shirt molded his shoulders. It was crumpled and creased as if he'd slept in it for days.

"Here you go." Tom placed the straw against her mouth and she sucked down some of the cool liquid. She wanted more but he pulled it away from her. "You shouldn't drink too much."

Her instinct was to grumble about it, but he was probably right. She had no idea how much time had passed or why she was in hospital. "Now will you tell me what happened? How long have I been here?"

Tom settled himself back in the chair he was

resting in when she woke up, bringing it closer to the bed. "You've been unconscious for three days," he said as he grabbed her hand. "You were poisoned."

Amberley had no idea what she'd been expecting, but to hear she'd been out for three days and had been poisoned wasn't it. She closed her eyes, willing her mind to give her a hint of what she'd done and what had happened before waking up in hospital.

In slow motion images coalesced behind her eyes. Her and Tom laughing in her kitchen. Them eating breakfast together. Then she was grabbing a box from him, opening it and pulling out the small statue of a woman writing. Her eyes flicked open. "The figurine?" she asked.

"Yeah. Whoever sent it to you covered it in poison. I guess they knew you'd run your fingers over it. They put a liberal amount on the notepad and pen.. You may not have had such a rapid reaction as you did if you hadn't cut your finger. It allowed the poison to travel through your system a lot faster."

Her mind whirled with all the information Tom was giving her. None of it really made sense to her. "Someone poisoned me? Who would do that?"

"That's the question we all want the answer to. I have so many question. I want to find and hurt the fucker who did this to you. But I won't because you just woke up."

Tom's demeanor had switched from concerned boyfriend to deadly Navy Seal. He was correct. At the moment her brain was way too fuzzy to be answering questions as to who may have done this to her. "What type of poison reacts so quickly with a simple touch?"

"Looks like a combination of secretions from poisonous frogs, but trust me when I say I've seen some scary stuff on my missions. Anything is possible these days, particularly with the dark web. People can get all sorts of shit from questionable people."

Amberley tightened her fingers around Tom's hand. Right now she didn't want to know what toxins had been in her system, all she cared about was that she was awake and alive. And the man she loved was right beside her.

Before she could say anything else the door was thrust open and her parents rushed into the room, quickly followed by a nurse. Tom released her hand and pushed his chair back in time for her mom to envelop her in a hug, uncaring of all the tubes that were attached to her.

"Amberley, you're awake. Thank God, I was so scared." Her mom then burst into tears. In all her life she could recall on one hand the times her mother cried. Her dad stood to the side, his hand resting on her mom's back. From where she lay she could also see the gleam of tears in his eyes.

After all her mom had put her through the last few months, setting her up on dates and shoving scripts under her nose, having her crying in her arms showed Amberley how much she meant to her parents.

Amberley closed her eyes and soaked up the love flowing from her parents. "I'm okay, Mom."

"I don't know what I would do if something happened to you. I love you, honey." Her mom kissed her cheek and stepped away to allow the nurse some room to do a quick examination.

"You're looking good, Ms. Price. I'll just go get the doctor so he can check you out." The nurse left the room and the second she did her father grabbed her hand.

"I love you too, sweetheart."

A throat clearing had her looking to her left and she spied Tom, a small smile playing across his lips. "I'll give you all some privacy."

He left before she could ask him to stay, but she appreciated the fact he was giving her a chance to speak to her parents.

The second he walked away her mom smiled at her. "When they transferred you to this room after they treated you, the only time he left your side was when we insisted he go get something to eat or stretch his legs. And even then we had to almost push him out the door" Her mom commented as she sat down in the chair Tom had been sitting in. "I was wrong about him."

Bettina Price admitting she'd made a mistake? She mustn't have heard her mom correctly. Bettina was always right, even when Amberley had known full well her mom was wrong. Admitting she'd been wrong about Tom was huge for her mother to acknowledge.

"How were you wrong, Mom?" she asked interested to see what she was going to say.

Her Mom leaned over and brushed her fingers across her forehead, as if pushing way stray strands of hair. "I thought I knew who the best partner to travel through life with you was. A man who worked in the same industry as us made total sense to me. But over the last three days I've seen who Thomas Grant is, and he's nothing like the men I introduced you too. He's better than them." She took a deep breath and smiled. "Not one of those men I forced upon you would've sat in this uncomfortable chair for three days. Slept in it. They'd have been out the door the second something happened to you. Not Thomas, he was the one who worked out what was wrong with you. Demanded the doctor be given the statue. If it wasn't for him," her voice hitched but she straightened her shoulders before continuing. "Well let's just say things would've been very different."

Amberley took a few moments to process everything Mom said to her. Had she just given Tom her seal of approval? It didn't surprise her to hear that Tom had slept by her side. She knew she would've done exactly the same if the roles had been reversed. It was what you did for people you loved. And there was no doubt she loved Tom Grant with her whole heart.

"I love him, Mom. You'll probably think it's too soon and impossible, but..." Her mom laid a hand on Amberley's arm.

"I knew the second your father stepped onto the set that he was for me." She looked over at her husband and Amberley couldn't believe the softening of her mom's expression. She'd never seen her mom look at her dad that way. His look mirrored her mom's. "He didn't succumb easily, I had to work hard to make him notice me. But when he did, I had no plans on giving him up. So you won't get any judgment from me as to how soon you and Tom fell in love."

Mom was jumping the gun a bit. Amberley knew he cared about her. Guilt may have kept him by her side the last three days. "I don't know that he loves me, Mom."

"Oh honey, no man would act the way Tom has acted the last three days if he didn't love you. Trust me. I know the signs."

Tiredness swept over her and it was getting harder and harder to keep her eyes open. "I think I need to sleep now, Mom."

As her eyes drifted shut she hoped her Mom spoke the truth and Tom loved her, because if he didn't her heart would never recover.

Tom closed his eyes and rested his head against the glass window of the fifth floor waiting room. He hadn't spent much time in the space since Amberley had been moved from the ICU to a normal room once she'd started responding to treatment. It had been late in the evening the first night she'd been admitted. He'd spent all of his time sitting by Amberley's side, willing her to wake up.

When her parents insisted he leave the room to eat or take a walk, he'd been so worried that the second he left she'd take a turn for the worse. Like when he was on a mission, he rushed through eating his food so that he could get back to Amberley.

A hand touched his shoulder and instinctively he turned and grabbed the wrist. His heart pounded in his chest, angry that he hadn't been paying attention to his surroundings, leaving him vulnerable to a surprise attack.

"Shit, Red, settle down. It's me, Robot." His team lead took a step back, holding his arms up in the universal sign of surrender.

The fight drained out of Tom as recognition sunk in. "Fuck, Robot, you should know better than to creep up behind me."

"Sorry, dude, we called your name like three times and thought you heard us."

Tom looked over Robot's shoulder and noticed Antonia, Cowboy and Faith standing behind him. "What are you guys doing here?"

The next second he was engulfed in a hug from Antonia. "Where else would we be? You need us and so here we are." She took a step back and Robot slid an arm around her waist, before kissing the top of her head. "The others would've been here too, but Brielle's blood pressure is high so her doctor doesn't want her flying and Emma and Kieran are teething so Suzie and Erin didn't think taking a long flight would be an enjoyable experience for anyone. So of course, that meant that Joker and Italy would stay home with them."

"I, uh, thanks. I didn't expect you guys to come all the way here. What if we get called to go on a mission?"

"Commander Black knows where we are and why. If there's a crisis he'll get one of the teams to cover it."

Tom rubbed a hand over his head, still shocked to see his team mates and their partners in the room with him. "Right. Well thanks for coming. I appreciate it." He turned back and resumed gazing out the window. He could hear the murmuring of the couples talking to each other and he figured it wouldn't be long before Robot was back by his side. It was what made him a good leader, knowing when to speak and when to act. Keeping his gaze fixed on the horizon he sensed Robot beside him.

"How's Amberley?"

"She's awake. Woke up about twenty minutes ago. I left her so she could spend some time with her parents. They needed to see for themselves that she was okay."

"Any idea who did this and why?"

Tom clenched his fists at his side. "I don't know why anyone would want to hurt her. It's not like she's been auditioning for any roles so a fellow author wanted her out of the picture. She's been concentrating on starting her career as a screenwriter and writing the script for this new movie."

"What about a competing writer? Someone pissed that she got the job and they didn't?"

Tom shrugged. "Maybe, but I don't think so. She never mentioned anything about anyone else being up for the job."

The questions Robot was asking weren't any different to the ones he'd asked himself as he'd sat by her bed, watching her breathe. The steady rise and fall of her chest had reassured him that she was still with him.

"How about an ex? Anyone in her past that would be upset she's seeing you?" This question came from Antonia who'd come to stand next to her husband. Once the two of them had gotten their heads out of their asses and worked out they loved each other, they didn't like to be too far away from the other.

"Again, not something we talked about. In fact her mom...fuck, why didn't I think of this before?" How could he have forgotten that important piece of information.

"Think of what, Red? What have you remembered," Robot questioned

Tom faced his team lead. "When Ambs, first came to see me in Virginia she told me that her mom was continually setting her up on dinner dates. She said that one guy didn't take the hint when she told him she wasn't interested. He only backed away when she threatened him with a restraining order."

"Do you know his name? Maybe we could get Tex to look into him?" Robot asked.

Frustration that he couldn't answer a simple question built in him. "Nah, she didn't say and I don't think she told her mom either, so she won't know who the guy is. Besides, as far as I know, the guy has been keeping his distance."

"You don't know that," piped up Antonia. "She may not have got around to saying anything to you about it. You did say that it was the morning after you arrived that she collapsed. I'm assuming you guys were too busy getting reacquainted the night before to talk about whether creepy dude was annoying her again."

Heat suffused his cheeks and he couldn't believe he was blushing in front of two of his teammates and their partners.

"Ohh is that how you got your nickname?" Antonia asked laughing when she noticed his blush. He swore his cheeks got redder.

"T, leave him alone," Robot said and pulled her closer to his side.

"Tom? Who are all these people?"

Tom swiveled and spied Bettina and John standing in the doorway.

"Oh my God, you're Bettina and John Price." Faith gushed excitedly. "I love all your movies. You're both so fabulous."

Bettina acknowledged Faith's praise with a slight nod. "Thank you." She turned her gaze to Tom's again and raised her eyebrow, clearly seeking an answer to her question.

"Bettina, John, these are two of my teammates, Robot—ah—Brendan and his wife Antonia." Tom indicated to his team lead. "And this is Cow—Greg and Faith."

The couples exchanged pleasantries but seeing Bettina and John in the room had him itching to go back to Amberley's side. It didn't matter that she'd woken up and appeared to not have any side effects from her ordeal, there was still a chance she could relapse. Not to mention the fucker who poisoned her in the first place was still lurking around. After talking to Robo and Antonia, he had a lead on who that person may be.

"Bettina, do you know the name of the guy who wouldn't leave Amberley alone? The one who she had to threaten with a restraining order for him to finally back off." Tom tried to keep the anger out of his voice but at Bettina's raised eyebrows he figured he hadn't succeeded.

"Steady, Red, you don't want to get on her bad side." Robot hissed out of the corner of his mouth.

Bettina lifted her chin, every inch the Hollywood A-List actress. "I have no idea what you're talking about, Thomas."

As he suspected, Amberley hadn't said anything to her mom about the situation. In her mother's eyes all the guys she set her daughter up with were upstanding citizens. He needed answers though and if he had to lay it out for her to understand he would.

He kept his gaze trained on the actress. "One of the guys you set your daughter up with wouldn't leave her alone. Wouldn't accept it when she told him she wasn't interested. She had to block his number numerous times and eventually told him if he didn't back off she'd get a restraining order against him." Tom explained everything again.

Bettina looked at her husband, her brows drawn down in confusion. "I really don't know what you're talking about. Amberley hasn't breathed a word of this to me. If she had I would make sure whoever this person was never worked a day in Hollywood."

Tom didn't doubt that she would follow through on her threat. She had enough power in Hollywood to make it happen, which was exactly why the guy probably had backed off.

"Do you think he's the one who hurt our daughter?" asked John.

Tom shrugged. "I don't know. I don't even know if he's contacted Amberley recently. But after," he pointed to his team lead. "Talking things through, it hit me that this guy could be considered a person of interest."

"Well don't go barreling into Amberley's room demanding answers. She went back to sleep," Bettina said, crossing her arms over her chest—mama bear was in the house. "And the doctor was going in as we walked out."

"I wouldn't do that to her, but I'm going back to sit with her." He looked over at Cowboy and Robot. "You guys staying at a hotel?"

"Yeah, we'll head there now. Text us when you find anything out and we'll do whatever we can to try and find this guy and get to the bottom of who hurt Amberley." Robot confirmed.

"Will do and thanks again for coming out here. I appreciate it."

Cowboy walked up to him. "You dropped everything to help me when I needed you. It's what we do. We're family."

The girls gave him a hug and the quartet said

goodbye to the Prices before disappearing out the door.

"Is that true?" John enquired once it was just them in the waiting room.

"Is what true?" Tom responded, eager to get back to Amberley's side.

"That you guys will drop everything when one of you needs help?"

"Absolutely. We're more than just team mates. As Cowboy said, we're family. We have to rely on each other when we're on missions and if anyone needs anything when we're back in the States, we're always the first ones there to help. No matter what it is. If it's painting a house, putting together baby furniture or getting our women out of trouble, we answer the call."

"That's extraordinary," John said shaking his head, clearly bemused at the idea of people willingly helping each other. Tom supposed in the cutthroat world of Hollywood that working together as a team was an anomaly.

"Are you saying that if Amberley stays with you, if she needs anything at all or gets into any type of trouble, all she has to do is call someone from your team and they'll be there?" This question came from Bettina, who had the same befuddled look on her face as her husband.

Repeating himself should have annoyed him, but he would say it thirty times if it would reassure the Prices that Amberley was safe with him.

Taking a deep breath, he laid everything out in the open. "Bettina, John, I love your daughter. I know I'm not the type of guy you wanted to see her with. I'm not from your world. I can't help her advance her career. But I will support her in what she wants to do with her life, even if she wants to go back into acting, or continue writing scripts. Whatever she wants I'll be right by her side and will do whatever is necessary to keep her safe. Anything she needs I'll make sure she gets it. And yes, my team and their partners will do the same. They'll be there if and when she needs it. No questions asked."

Bettina moved forward and he waited to see what she was going to do next. When she reached up and touched his cheek, he tensed for half a heartbeat before relaxing. "As I told Amberley, I was wrong about you. I can see that now. You're everything I've been looking for in a man to love my daughter. And I know that what you feel for her is real and not as a way to get in good with us. I trust..." She paused and looked at her husband who smiled lovingly at her. "No, *we* trust that you will keep our daughter safe."

And just like that, Tom was aware that he'd been given their seal of approval. "Thank you."

"You're welcome, and now go, I know you're itching to get back to our daughter," John canted his head toward the door.

"Yes, sir, I am." With a chin lift he left the couple behind, a spring in his step. Now that he knew her parents had no issue with them being together, he planned to convince Amberley that they were meant to be together.

CHAPTER TWELVE

Amberley jolted awake when the hand closed over her mouth. Her heart beat loudly in her ears, matching the rapid increase of the beeping from the heart monitor. She'd drifted in and out of sleep while the doctor examined her.

Her eyes widened as recognition set in. Simon Wilson stood over her, a maniacal smile on his face. "I'm sorry it had to come to this, my sweet Amberley. If you'd just continued to date me, none of this would be necessary. We could've been the darlings of Hollywood, just like your parents. Now be a good girl and don't scream when I remove my hand, otherwise..." He lifted his hand, the light glittered off the polished silver of a knife blade. "I'm going to have to scar you and I don't want to do that. We won't be able to get roles opposite each other. No one wants to hire a scarred actress."

A shiver of fear rippled through her when he ran the blade down her cheek. If she moved her head to get away from the tip, it could dig in and cut her. Weakness still pervaded every inch of her body so there was no way she'd be able to fight him off, and how she wanted to.

As if sensing that she was going to go along with everything he wanted Simon lifted his hand away, but he kept the knife close to her face.

He lifted his hand and she sucked in a deep breath. "Now, that's a good girl. Did you like the figurine I sent you? It's my way of being supportive of this little dream you have of being a screenwriter. But I know acting is where your talents really lie."

The guy had absolutely no idea who she was and what her dreams were. Another reason why she never considered dating him.

"That statue made me sick, you asshole." The words burst out of her and the second he dug the knife into her cheek she cursed herself for not thinking about what she said.

"Now. Now. That wasn't a very nice thing to say." With his free hand he stroked down her arm. She couldn't stop the shiver of revulsion flowing through her. "I didn't want to hurt you, Amberley. But you kept ignoring my calls, I had to make you sit up and notice."

Amberley wanted to scream to get someone's attention. Where had her parents gone, they'd been there when she'd fallen asleep. Where was Tom? Had he left? Had he gone home? Why would he leave when her mom said he hadn't left her side since she'd been brought in?

None of this made sense, especially Simon's decree that he thought they would be like her parents. She knew if her mind still wasn't hazy, she'd be able to handle this situation a little better. Perhaps if she kept him talking long enough, then Tom would come back and save her. He could go all Navy Seal on him.

"Simon, if you wanted us to be the same as my parents, why did you try and kill me?"

The press of the metal against her cheek lessened a little and Simon's features softened, his eyes took on an almost friendly slant and his mouth relaxed into a smile. "Oh, my sweet Amberley, it was never supposed to put you in hospital. I only wanted to make you a little sick. I spent the whole night hidden in your garden waiting to come and rescue you. But you had that man in your house all night." He spat the words out and dug the knife back in. "The guy who wouldn't leave your side from the moment they brought you here. I've been waiting and waiting to get close to you. I wanted to be the one to rescue you. I wanted you to look at me as your savior. You'd be so thankful that I saved you that you'd fall in love with me."

The longer he spoke, the more unstable he became. Fear gnawed at her and she wished she had the strength to get out of the bed and make a run for it.

Where was Tom? Why hadn't he come back to the room? How long had she been asleep? How long ago did her parents leave? They said Tom never left her side. Had Simon done something to them all before he came into her room?

Amberley squashed those thoughts, she couldn't let them take over. She had to try and keep a cool head in an impossible situation.

Something niggled in her mind. Something that he said that stood out to her. "How did you manage to get past security at the house?"

Amberley was well aware her parents had cameras all around her property, not to mention the guards on duty 24/7. As for now, in the hospital, she was in a regular room so they probably weren't screening her visitors. Then again even if they were, Simon would probably sweet talk his way in somehow.

"Oh you'd be surprised how easy it was to get

onto your parents property. I just hid in the bushes and when they opened the gate for the delivery guy, I used the cover of the van to slip in. It was dark after all and I was wearing all black. And to think your parents scoffed at me the night we had dinner when I told them I could be the next James Bond."

Amberley recalled that conversation. She'd agreed with her parents thinking he wouldn't be a good James Bond. His British accent was atrocious but it seemed he did have some stealth skills.

"You know that by poisoning me you've wrecked your career? No one will want anything to do with you now. Once the press get a hold of this your name will be blacklisted all over Hollywood. That is if my mom doesn't do it when she finds out what you've done. Not to mention you'll go to prison of attempting to kill me."

"Shut up," he yelled at her. He leaned closer and she could see his pupils were dilated. He looked like he was flying high and clearly her words had gotten to him. He dug the knife deeper again and this time she felt the sting of it cutting her flesh. "You know nothing. Nothing at all. You mom will never say anything, I'll make sure of it."

Movement over his right shoulder caught her and she spied Tom standing in the doorway. She wanted to cry out in relief but he shook his head and held a finger up to this lips in the universal sign of quiet.

Everything about him screamed lethal weapon. If she didn't know him she'd be running in the opposite direction. His face looked like it was carved out of granite. His eyes were narrowed and if they could shoot bullets, they'd be spraying the man leaning over her.

"Now look what you made me do to you, Amberley," Simon whined as he continued to lean over her. "I didn't want to hurt you and now I have. Why can't you see what's right in front of you. How perfect we are for each other. I don't understand what you see in that jerk that spent the night at your place. He's nothing. A nobody. What can he give you that I can't."

The answer was so easy, she didn't even have to think long about it. "Safety," she said simply. "He can keep me safe."

Simon laughed at her. "Right. If he can keep you safe, where is he right now."

"I'm right behind you, asshole." Tom spoke with deadly intent.

Simon whirled around and before he could even raise his knife Tom throat punched him and then swung his leg, knocking Simon's own legs from beneath him. The look of surprise on Simon's face would've been almost comical if relief wasn't slamming into her knowing that Tom hadn't deserted her and left her to this psycho. As Simon fell to the ground his head slammed on the side of the bed, jolting the bed so violently it skidded across the floor a little way.

Tom spared him a cursory look before he rushed to her side, wrapping her up in his arms. The second his warmth surrounded her she closed her eyes and rested against him.

"Thank God, you're okay. I don't know what I would've done if he'd hurt you, Ambs." He framed her face encouraging her to open her eyes. Her breath caught when their gazes collided. "I love you Amberley Price. I've had a crush on you since the first day you walked into my house with my sister. I don't ever want to be apart from you again. I know you live here and I live in Virginia, but we'll make it work somehow."

Beyond his shoulder she was vaguely aware of security coming into the room to take care of Simon. She ignored them. The man holding her was all that mattered. "I love you too, Thomas Grant. I've had a crush on you as long as you've had one on me. I don't want to be apart from you either. I can write anywhere and I think I've proven I can write well in Virginia. Just so long as you're near me I'll be happy."

A huge smile broke out over his face, chasing away any remaining shadows of doubt inside her of her future was with this man. “Sounds perfect to me.”

Needing to affirm her feelings for him and have that physical connection she tugged his head down to hers. Before their lips met she smiled up at him. “I love you, Thomas Grant.”

“And I love you, Amberley Price.

CHAPTER THIRTEEN

Amberley snuggled into Tom's side and listened as he and Cowboy talked about the latest football game. His arm tightened around her and he dropped a kiss on her head before continuing his conversation.

The whole team and their partners were spending the afternoon at Robot's place. They'd also been joined by two of their former teammates and their partners. An impromptu party to celebrate hers and Tom's engagement. She glanced at the emerald on her left hand, the stone sparkling in the sunlight. Both their parents had been over the moon when they'd called them that morning to share the news.

Now they were with Tom's other family and Amberley was honored to be part of it. The partners of Tom's teammates had welcomed her as if she'd always been there.

She couldn't wait to spend more time with them now that she was finally in Virginia. She and Tom were about to close on a house and she couldn't wait to make it their own.

It had been three months since her poisoning. Simon had been evaluated by the psych ward at the hospital and admitted into a facility. At the moment, he wasn't mentally capable of standing trial to face the charges of attempted murder.

The outcome had made Tom angry and she'd had to kiss him senseless until he calmed down. Her body warmed as she remembered just what they'd gotten up to.

"I recognize that smile." Amberley looked up and found Erin standing in front of her, baby Kieran propped on her hip.

"What type of smile is that?" Suzie asked as she walked up holding her daughter, Emma.

"The type we can't discuss around the guys." Antonia joined the group. "Come on Amberley, it's time all us girls had a chat. Not to mention plan a wedding"

"Uh oh, this is going to be dangerous, go gentle on her T. Amberley's just moved here Don't scare her away. Red won't forgive you if you do that." Robot dropped a kiss on his wife's cheek.

Antonia rolled her eyes, and Amberley couldn't help but laugh at their antics. The couple were entertaining to say the least. But their love couldn't be denied.

Amberley stood and eyeballed Robot. "It's okay, I think I can hold my own. I did grow up in Hollywood, you know."

The guys hooted with laughter and Robot inclined his head toward her. "Don't say I didn't warn you." He finished with a wink.

Before she could make a move toward where all the girls were congregated, Tom reached and touched her arm. She glanced over her shoulder. "If you need me, just let me know," he murmured.

Her heart somersaulted at his sweet gesture. "You betcha." She leaned down and kissed him on the lips. When she went to pull away his hand curled around the back of her head, preventing her from going. Her mouth opened beneath his and his tongue dueled with hers. She moaned deep in her throat and she wanted to rip his clothes off and feast on his body.

Slowly the sound of catcalls and whistles permeated her consciousness and she pulled away from Tom. He kept his hand anchored around her neck and rested his forehead against hers.

"You know the girls are going to give me even more of a hard time now," she complained.

Tom laughed. "Trust me, it's nothing they haven't done before. You should've seen the arguments Robot and Antonia had in front of all of us before they got together."

Amberley shook her head and pulled away from him, turning to face the group of women who all had huge smiles on their faces. She shrugged her shoulders. "What can I say, he's insecure sometimes, even though I said yes to his proposal."

Everyone burst out laughing. Yeah, it was really good to be part of a team.

EPILOGUE

Samantha Rayse, also known as Samantha Jackson, looked at the picture of her brother and sister, their respective partners and Rayne's baby. How she wanted to be able to go visit them. Spend time getting to know the gorgeous baby in the photo. Laughing with her brother and sister and their partners.

God, she missed them so much, but regardless of the fact that Rayne's husband, Ghost, was a Delta Force soldier and Chase was a soldier too, keeping her distance from them would keep them safe. She was the oldest and it was her job to make sure nothing bad happened to them. If that meant she couldn't see them, then so be it.

She had to keep them safe.

Placing the photo down on her coffee table, she

wished that things could be different. The only high point in her life was that her career was taking off, she'd landed the lead female role in a major motion picture and filming was due to start the next day.

Being on set surrounded by people would keep her safe, wouldn't it?

If you enjoyed this book please consider leaving a review. All reviews are greatly appreciated.

JOIN my Newsletter and find out about sales, free books, contests and new releases before anyone else! Click HERE

You can read where the "Guardian Seals" all started with Protecting Lily. Click HERE

If you enjoy hot doctors, paramedics and sassy, independent nurses, check out my "Lovers Unmasked" series. Grab the first book, Masquerade HERE

To find out about new releases and sales follow me on Bookbub. Follow me

ABOUT THE AUTHOR

On her very first school report her teacher said 'Nicole likes to tell her own stories'. Many years later she eventually sat down and wrote her first book.

Nicole writes sexy contemporary romances, seducing you one kiss at a time as you turn the pages. She enjoys taking two characters and creating unique situations for them.

When she's not writing, she's busy spreading glitter over social media and having a ton of fun doing it.

Learn more about Nicole Flockton at http://www.nicoleflockton.com.

authornicole@nicoleflockton.com

ALSO BY NICOLE FLOCKTON

Guardian Seals

Protecting Lily

Protecting Maria

Guarding Erin

Guarding Suzie

Guarding Brielle

Guarding Antonia

Guarding Faith

Guarding Amberley

Man's Best Friend

Blind Date Bet

Next Door Knight

The Matchmaker's Match

Lovers Unmasked Series

Masquerade

Rescuing Dawn

Seducing Phoebe

The Elite

Fighting to Win

Fighting to Dream

Fighting for Love

Fighting for Redemption

The Freemasons

The Victor

The Hunter

Bound Series

Bound by Her Ring

Bound by His Desire

Bound by Their Love

Bound by The Billionaire's Desire - Boxed Set

Emerald Springs Legacy Series

Daniel's Decision

Emerald Springs Legacy Collection

Barefoot Bay

Swipe for Mr. Right

Wrong Time for Mr. Right

Novellas

Tangled Vines

Tango Love

A Vacation Affair

Christmas in Ghost Gum Valley

There are many more books in this fan fiction world than listed here, for an up-to-date list go to www.AcesPress.com

You can also visit our Amazon page at: http://www.amazon.com/author/operationalpha

Special Forces: Operation Alpha World

Denise Agnew: Dangerous to Hold
Shauna Allen: Awakening Aubrey
Shauna Allen: Defending Danielle
Shauna Allen: Rescuing Rebekah
Shauna Allen: Saving Scarlett
Shauna Allen: Saving Grace
Brynne Asher: Blackburn
Jennifer Becker: Hiding Catherine
Julia Bright: Saving Lorelei
Julia Bright: Rescuing Amy
Victoria Bright: Surviving Savage
Victoria Bright: Going Ghost
Victoria Bright: Jostling Joker
Cara Carnes: Protecting Mari
Kendra Mei Chailyn: Beast
Kendra Mei Chailyn: Barbie
Kendra Mei Chailyn : Pitbull
Melissa Kay Clarke: Rescuing Annabeth

Melissa Kay Clarke: Safeguarding Miley
Samantha A. Cole: Handling Haven
Samantha A. Cole: Cheating the Devil
Sue Coletta: Hacked
Melissa Combs: Gallant
KaLyn Cooper: Rescuing Melina
Liz Crowe: Marking Mariah
Jordan Dane: Redemption for Avery
Jordan Dane: Fiona's Salvation
Riley Edwards: Protecting Olivia
Riley Edwards: Redeeming Violet
Riley Edwards, Recovering Ivy
Nicole Flockton: Protecting Maria
Nicole Flockton: Guarding Erin
Nicole Flockton: Guarding Suzie
Nicole Flockton: Guarding Brielle
Casey Hagen: Shielding Nebraska
Casey Hagen: Shielding Harlow
Casey Hagen: Shielding Josie
Casey Hagen: Shielding Blair
Desiree Holt: Protecting Maddie
Kathy Ivan: Saving Sarah
Kathy Ivan: Saving Savannah
Kathy Ivan: Saving Stephanie
Jesse Jacobson: Protecting Honor
Jesse Jacobson: Fighting for Honor

Jesse Jacobson: Defending Honor
Jesse Jacobson: Summer Breeze
Silver James: Rescue Moon
Silver James: SEAL Moon
Silver James: Assassin's Moon
Silver James: Under the Assassin's Moon
Becca Jameson: Saving Sofia
Kate Kinsley: Protecting Ava
Heather Long: Securing Arizona
Heather Long: Guarding Gertrude
Heather Long: Protecting Pilar
Heather Long: Covering Coco
Gennita Low: No Protection
Kirsten Lynn: Joining Forces for Jesse
Margaret Madigan: Bang for the Buck
Margaret Madigan: Buck the System
Margaret Madigan: Jungle Buck
Margaret Madigan: December Chill
Rachel McNeely: The SEAL's Surprise Baby
Rachel McNeely: The SEAL's Surprise Bride
Rachel McNeely: The SEAL's Surprise Twin
KD Michaels: Saving Laura
KD Michaels: Protecting Shane
KD Michaels: Avenging Angels
Wren Michaels: The Fox & The Hound
Wren Michaels: The Fox & The Hound 2

Wren Michaels: Shadow of Doubt
Wren Michaels: Shift of Fate
Wren Michaels: Steeling His Heart
Kat Mizera: Protecting Bobbi
Mary B Moore: Force Protection
LeTeisha Newton: Protecting Butterfly
LeTeisha Newton: Protecting Goddess
LeTeisha Newton: Protecting Vixen
LeTeisha Newton: Protecting Heartbeat
MJ Nightingale: Protecting Beauty
MJ Nightingale: Betting on Benny
MJ Nightingale: Protecting Secrets
Sarah O'Rourke: Saving Liberty
Debra Parmley: Protecting Pippa
Lainey Reese: Protecting New York
Jenika Snow: Protecting Lily
Jen Talty: Burning Desire
Jen Talty: Burning Kiss
Jen Talty: Burning Skies
Jen Talty: Burning Lies
Jen Talty: Burning Heart
Megan Vernon: Protecting Us
Megan Vernon: Protecting Earth

Police and Fire: Operation Alpha World

Freya Barker: Burning for Autumn
KaLyn Cooper: Justice for Gwen

MORE SPECIAL FORCES: OPERATION ALPHA WORLD BOOKS

Aspen Drake: Sheltering Emma

Deanndra Hall: Shelter for Sharla

Deanndra Hall:Justice for Aleta

Barb Han: Kace

Reina Torres: Justice for Sloane

Stacey Wilk: Stage Fright

As you know, this book included at least one character from Susan Stoker's books. To check out more, see below.

SEAL of Protection: Legacy Series

Securing Caite

Securing Brenae (novella)

Securing Sidney

Securing Piper (Aug 2019)

Securing Zoey (Jan 2020)

Securing Avery (May 2020)

Securing Kalee (Sept 2020)

Delta Force Heroes Series

Rescuing Rayne (FREE!)

Rescuing Aimee (novella)

Rescuing Emily

Rescuing Harley

Marrying Emily (novella)

Rescuing Kassie

Rescuing Bryn

Rescuing Casey

Rescuing Sadie (novella)

Rescuing Wendy

Rescuing Mary

Rescuing Macie (Novella)

Badge of Honor: Texas Heroes Series

Justice for Mackenzie (FREE!)
Justice for Mickie
Justice for Corrie
Justice for Laine (novella)
Shelter for Elizabeth
Justice for Boone
Shelter for Adeline
Shelter for Sophie
Justice for Erin
Justice for Milena
Shelter for Blythe
Justice for Hope
Shelter for Quinn
Shelter for Koren (July 2019)
Shelter for Penelope (Oct 2019)

SEAL of Protection Series

Protecting Caroline (FREE!)
Protecting Alabama
Protecting Fiona
Marrying Caroline (novella)
Protecting Summer
Protecting Cheyenne
Protecting Jessyka
Protecting Julie (novella)
Protecting Melody

Protecting the Future
Protecting Kiera (novella)
Protecting Alabama's Kids (novella)
Protecting Dakota

New York Times, *USA Today* and *Wall Street Journal* Bestselling Author Susan Stoker has a heart as big as the state of Tennessee where she lives, but this all American girl has also spent the last fourteen years living in Missouri, California, Colorado, Indiana, and Texas. She's married to a retired Army man who now gets to follow *her* around the country.

She debuted her first series in 2014 and quickly followed that up with the SEAL of Protection Series, which solidified her love of writing and creating stories readers can get lost in.

If you enjoyed this book, or any book, please consider leaving a review. It's appreciated by authors more than you'll know.

www.stokeraces.com
www.AcesPress.com
susan@stokeraces.com

Made in United States
Cleveland, OH
05 March 2026

34168837R00118